To Heather "the Hammer" Ludviksson, Katherine "Cupcakes" Sears, and the rest of my Booktrope family. There was a time when I thought seeing my books in print was going to be the best part of being a published author. Now I realize it's the friends I've made on the journey.

You are my colleagues, my champions, my friends. I'm honored to know you.

ROSES IN ECUADOR

HEATHER HUFFMAN

booktrope

Booktrope Editions
Seattle WA 2013

Cover Design by Emily Stoltz-Spitz

Edited by Erica Fitzgerald

This is a work of fiction. Names, characters, places, brands, media, and incidents are either the product of the author's imagination or are used fictitiously. Any resemblance to similarly named places or to persons living or deceased is unintentional.

PRINT ISBN 978-1-935961-53-6
EPUB ISBN 978-1-62015-057-3

For further information regarding permissions, please contact info@booktrope.com.

Library of Congress Control Number: 2013930316

CHAPTER ONE

THE BOY'S DARK BROWN EYES soaked in the flurry of activity going on in the distance. From his vantage point in the jungle, he saw the pretty blonde race to get the middle-aged Hispanic man. The teenager had seen these two many times before; he often watched them when he was on lookout. It was a boring job, somehow made more bearable watching this unlikely pair and wondering who they were and how they'd both come to be here.

But more than the people who came and went from this place, what Eduardo loved most about his post was watching the cats. When he was a little boy, his grandfather had told him stories about the great cats that shared their forest, but it had been many years since anyone had seen one of the elusive creatures. Many said the beasts were gone forever. Some said that was a good thing; that the cats were a threat to livestock. Others worried that the balance of the rainforest would be lost without its most majestic predator.

Personally, Eduardo was happy that the American had come to help bring back the cats. He loved watching them, loved knowing the forest around him was once again in balance.

He pulled out his binoculars, trying to figure out just what was going on down there. A smile played on his lips when the blonde did a silly little dance; it seemed so out of character for her. Then he saw the source of her joy and his grin widened. One of the jaguars had two new cubs.

He could have sat there for hours, watching the new life and the celebration it caused, but a twig broke in the distance, alerting him that his relief had shown up. His shift was over.

"Anything new?" Creases around the man's eyes showed that he was much older than Eduardo and that his years had been spent in the sun.

Eduardo shook his head tersely. His colleague wouldn't appreciate jaguar cubs. It was unlikely there would ever be anything else going on. Eduardo's watch point was the farthest distance from the factory or their transport routes. He was the last stop before a jaguar preserve and a flower plantation, and neither of those was known for their excitement. "Anything new back at base?"

"There's talk of finding a new road out. DEA is sniffing around the usual routes."

"I thought they'd been paid."

"So did Javier. Keep your head down when you check in. He's in a mood."

"Thanks for the warning." Eduardo rose to leave, casting a glance over his shoulder at the pretty blonde as she bent down to inspect the new cubs. His stomach clenched with dread. He had a feeling where Javier's new road would lead.

CHAPTER TWO

JANE RUSSELL SCANNED THE ROOM, her green eyes looking for an escape. Her ability to breathe was seriously hampered by the crushing feeling in her chest. Humidity clung to the air, forming beads of sweat on her skin.

Not 100 feet away, the open air of the jungle beckoned her. She knew if she could make it that far, she would be rewarded by the distant call of a macaw and the chatter of night monkeys. She might, if the wind was right, even catch the gentle fragrance of roses drifting on the breeze.

Jane knew she was being watched, though. She could feel the weight of the stare, but in the current throng, she couldn't find the source of it.

Outwardly, she carried on a conversation with her companions. Mentally, she debated her chances of covering the distance to sweet freedom.

CHAPTER THREE

DEVON MCALISTER WATCHED THE PRETTY BLONDE from across the open-air bar in the heart of the little Ecuadorian village in the center of the Amazon Basin. He tried in vain to remember what color her eyes were, then wondered why he cared. Maybe it was something about the way wisps of curls escaped their binding to frame her delicate face. More than likely, he was forced to admit, it was the complete apathy she showed him. That wasn't a sentiment he was used to garnering from anyone.

Even now, she seemed completely oblivious to his presence as she chatted with her friends. Occasionally, her eyes would flit about the room as if she were looking for something or someone. Maybe she could feel the weight of his gaze, and it was him she sought.

From what the locals said about her, there was no way she was looking for a man. Some rumored that she hailed from a convent and likened her to Mother Theresa. Others swore she simply had ice in her veins, though the latter sentiment often came from poachers who'd made the mistake of wandering onto the stretch of Amazon Basin in her care.

He watched her cheeks flush as the table around her erupted in laughter and knew neither rumor was true. Still, why had the pretty young teacher from Arkansas moved to a jaguar preserve in Ecuador, especially one that was under constant threat from local farmers?

He wanted to approach her but was rooted to his spot by an unusual feeling: uncertainty. Devon was only vaguely aware of the conversations floating around him. His mind was too busy trying to solve the puzzle of Jane Russell.

She rose from her chair, waving off those who would follow. He knew if he wanted to approach her without an audience, this was his moment. As he wound his way through the crush of people on the dance floor, he wondered what he would say to her. There was no way to make this look like a casual encounter.

"Jane," he called out when it looked like she was going to slip away.

She stopped and turned to him, her large green eyes giving away how startled she was by the sound of his voice.

"I'm Devon. Devon McAlister."

"I know." Her reply was clipped. She took a deep breath and smiled, her tone softening as she explained, "We're two of three *gringos* in this town."

"Right, well, I just wanted to formally introduce myself. You've been here a while; it doesn't seem neighborly that I haven't even come by to say hello."

"I wasn't worried about it."

"Oh, well...." He didn't have a response, yet another feeling he wasn't accustomed to.

"That probably sounded really rude. I'm so sorry. I think I've forgotten how to talk to people," she apologized, rubbing her fingers across her forehead as she did. "I just meant that I've heard you're a busy man, so I didn't think anything of you not stopping by."

"No offense taken." He found her mannerisms adorable.

"So, anyway... pleased to meet you." She extended a hand toward him. He enclosed it in his own, marveling at how dainty and smooth it felt in comparison to his own large, work-hardened hands.

He cleared his throat. "Pleased to meet you as well. Listen, if you ever need anything, I'm just right down the road from you."

"Thank you." Her voice was soft, like a caress.

"You're welcome." He was riveted.

"Devon?"

"Yes?"

"There is one thing I need." A grin twitched at the corner of her mouth.

"Anything." He flashed his dimples.

"My hand."

"Absolutely." He jumped back, his hands dropping self-consciously to his sides.

"Thank you." At that, her smile came out full force.

"I don't suppose you'd stick around long enough to get a drink with me?" Devon could see the hesitation in her eyes. He sensed rejection was coming on the heels of making a fool of himself. "If you have to get back, it's no big deal. Some other time."

"No, that's okay," she intercepted his hasty retreat. "I could stay for a few minutes. It's kind of creepy going back to the preserve alone at night anyway."

"Then why were you leaving?" he couldn't help asking as he held a seat out for her at the corner of the bar.

"Honestly?" she hesitated.

"Preferably, yes."

"I couldn't stand the meat market anymore," she blurted, wrapping both hands around the wine glass she'd been given and staring at her sangria.

"Excuse me?"

"The constant attempts to set me up." Her eyes flew to meet his. "I know my friends mean well, but I have zero interest in men right now."

"Why is that?" The words tumbled out of his mouth before he could assess their wisdom.

"Didn't you hear? I'm a nun."

"I thought that was just a rumor."

"It is. I'm not even Catholic, but the look on your face there for a second was pretty priceless."

"Why do people say you're a nun, Jane?" He lowered his voice and leaned in closer.

"Probably because I first came to Ecuador on an inter-denominational mission trip. There were several nuns with us at the time. Or maybe I just look like a nun. Do nuns have a certain look to them?"

He smiled at her musings but kept pressing in for more information. He felt no closer to solving the mystery of her. "How did a mission trip translate into working for the preserve?"

"I don't know." She shook her head. She licked her lips and furrowed her brow, as if trying to think it through. Devon found the gesture so fascinating he almost missed her next words. "There was just something so magical about this place. And then, completely by chance, I met Aldo and he told me about the work he'd been doing with the jaguars. When everyone else took a day off to go hiking, I went to tour the preserve instead."

"And?" Devon prompted, motioning the bartender to refill her glass.

"I fell in love." She shrugged before taking a sip of the fresh sangria. She sighed with approval. Devon felt a stab of jealousy before she continued. "There was this one jaguar in particular. They called her Deifilia. She was breathtaking – I had no idea how huge and powerful they would be in person."

"So, you just quit your job and moved?"

"Pretty much," she admitted. "The thought of going back home just seemed so… hollow. I guess that sounds silly."

"Not at all." He ached to reach out and touch her but had the distinct impression that the merest brush of her skin would send her running.

"I have no idea why I'm rambling on and on tonight." She closed her eyes and pressed her fingers to her forehead.

"It's the sangria," he guessed. "But you're not rambling. Tell me more."

"What do you want to know?"She cocked her head and smiled up at him.

"All of it."

"I haven't had that much sangria."

"Fine, start with what you do at the preserve. Weren't you a teacher before?"

"Word does get around, doesn't it?" she asked ruefully. "I was a biology teacher – that's actually what my degree was in, biology. I just got the teaching job because there weren't many career options in my hometown."

"So why didn't you leave sooner?"

"Next question." She shook her head.

"Are you glad you came?" He let her aversion to the question slide, mentally filing it away for later.

She calculated her answer. "Most days."

"What about the other days?"

"I guess I didn't realize how many people would be against the reintroduction of a native species."

"The farmers worry about their livestock."

"I know. I get it, but surely the basin is big enough for both." She paused to stab a piece of fruit at the bottom of her glass, sucking the wine off the orange slice before popping it in her mouth.

"Tell me more about Deifilia," he prompted, hoping he imagined the crack in his voice.

"She's magnificent," Jane replied wistfully, her eyes lighting up. "I could spend hours watching her with her cubs."

"Cubs? Sounds promising."

"She had two about three weeks ago. One has the classic spots and one is inky black. Both have me wrapped around their little paws."

"I'll have to ask them what their secret is sometime."

"Flirt," she accused, her soft laugh only stoking the flames that were starting to lap at his skin from her nearness.

"Would you like to dance?"

"No, thank you. I've never been much on dancing. I get a little claustrophobic in big crowds of people."

"I don't know what to make of that. My sister is addicted to dancing – I'm used to being dragged out on the floor every chance she gets." He leaned back, allowing himself to drink in some fresh air lest he drown in this delightfully perplexing woman.

"You have a sister?"

"Two, actually."

"I never would have guessed."

"Why is that?"

"I guess I just thought someone with sisters would respect women more."

"Ouch. You don't think I respect women?"

"I'm sorry. I, of all people, should know better than to listen to the rumor mill."

"And what is the rumor mill saying about me these days?" Devon delighted in the way her cheeks flushed prettily at his question.

"You probably know as well as I do what people say."

"What do you think?" He leaned in again, soaking in the delicious heat radiating off of her.

"I've seen you around the village. You're a bit of a magnet for beautiful women. I don't even know where you find them all."

"It's a gift."

Her laugh was still soft, yet this time it held a hint of derision. "I don't understand it."

"That stung a little."

She bit her lower lip and gave him a look of contrition. "Sorry. I didn't mean it to come out quite like that."

"You're a beautiful woman. You're having a drink with me. What's not to understand?"

"Oh no, I'm not one of your arm ornaments."

He tsked and shook his head. "So judgmental."

"I'm not judging." She frowned at him. "I'm just... judging. You're right."

"I won't tell if you won't." His promise was laced with potential meanings.

"I should probably go."

"I wish you wouldn't." Devon surprised himself at how much he meant it.

"But I should." She stood just as he did. When they bumped into each other, he seized the opportunity to touch her again, reaching out to steady her in a movement that was more of an embrace than the moment required.

"I've enjoyed this."

"Me, too." Her reply was breathless. Devon's hope surged that her reaction meant she was attracted to him.

"We should do it again." He wondered what she'd do if he kissed her right then and there.

"I don't think so. It would hurt my reputation back at the convent."

"What are you hiding from?" His words were barely above a whisper.

"Who says I'm hiding? Maybe I'm just not interested. And that's an awfully personal question."

"You're right. Forgive me." He was stunned by her complete lack of guile.

"Forgiven." The shy smile she blessed him with made him want to hold her all the tighter. Instead, she moved away, increasing the distance between them. "Thank you for the drinks."

"Next time, we dance," he vowed.

"There is no next time."

CHAPTER FOUR

JANE WONDERED IF ALDO AND MARIA GUERRERO could hear her heart pounding as they bumped along in their battered old pickup truck down the tiny dirt road that led home. They'd certainly noticed the flush to her cheeks, although Aldo's comment about it earned him a swat on the shoulder from his wife.

"Mr. McAlister seems like a nice man," Maria remarked.

"Mmm-hmmm," Jane murmured with a nod, her eyes barely leaving the window. She was struggling to wrap her brain around the myriad of emotions swirling through her, let alone hold a coherent conversation about the man.

Two short years ago she'd sworn off men for good. Tonight, she was appalled at her stunning lack of resolve, especially given that the man was an unrepentant heartbreaker. Still, when he'd put his arms around her to keep her from tumbling off her stool back at the bar, she'd almost convinced herself that one night with him would be worth the cost. Almost.

Even thinking about the pleasant feel of his hands around her waist sent her heart racing again. Surely her friends had to be able to hear that. Jane inhaled deeply in hopes of steadying herself, but the heady fragrance of roses flooded through her, bringing with it new thoughts of Devon McAlister. She wondered if a bed of roses would be as decadent as it sounded or just messy.

"I thought commercial roses weren't supposed to be fragrant," Jane pondered aloud, trying to distract herself from the mental image of trailing rose petals along Devon's tanned skin.

"I don't know about other plantations, but Mr. McAlister's roses smell lovely." Maria leaned out the window a little and took a deep breath. "I love when the wind carries their scent all the way to us."

"Me too." *Most of the time*, Jane mentally amended. Some moments, like this one, it wasn't exactly helping her get her mind off Devon.

"Maybe you can ask Mr. McAlister about his roses next time you see him," Aldo suggested, his tone sounding somewhat mischievous.

"You're not going to stop until I have a man, are you?" Jane laughed despite herself.

"No."

His answer was honest. Jane had to give him that. His genuine nature was one of the many things Jane respected about Aldo. Before meeting Aldo and Maria, she had begun to question whether there were any sincere people left on the planet. Well, besides her cousin Charlie and his family, but they'd moved away before she came to Ecuador, so she rarely saw them anymore. They probably would have let her follow them because they were nice, but it seemed a little pathetic and desperate to just tag along wherever they went.

The sangria she'd downed earlier was making her sleepy, or maybe it was simply that the rush of her encounter with Devon was beginning to wear off. Jane longed for her favorite pajamas and the comfort of her little bed.

As soon as the truck was parked, she headed to check on the animals one last time. Most of the animals on the preserve roamed freely over a large expanse of basin land, but a few were held in enclosures near the main compound because they needed extra care for one reason or another. Deifilia and her cubs were in the enclosure closest to Jane's own cabin.

On the nights when Jane couldn't sleep, she'd sit and watch the trio for hours at a time. She'd jot down notes and take pictures. The animals were used to her, which gave her the chance to see them behave as naturally as any human ever would. She documented every bit of it she could. One day she hoped to have enough of her experience written down to turn it into a book. Maybe then people would begin to understand what was happening in the Amazon and why it mattered in places like Arkansas and beyond.

Only it was going to take a lot of work to turn her ramblings into a book that anybody might care to read. As it stood now, it was more like a personal journal with scientific observations scattered throughout. Something about being in the presence of the cats allowed her to pour onto those pages all of the things she couldn't even admit to herself.

But tonight, she wasn't in the mood to watch the cats. Her thoughts were such a jumble, even the jaguars wouldn't help sort them out. Jane paused to watch Deifilia pace restlessly back and forth. "What's wrong, girl?"

Deifilia's response was a deep, chesty sound somewhat like a roar.

"I know the feeling," Jane empathized before heading to her cabin. She changed into her pajamas and climbed into bed, relishing the feel of the cool cotton sheets on her bare toes.

No matter how hard she tried or how badly she wanted to sleep, Jane couldn't seem to keep her mind from drifting back to her encounter with Devon. Why had he sought her out? Maybe there was a shortage of women in the jungle. Maybe he was tired of the easy catch and decided to go for a challenge.

That thought made Jane frown. She had no intention of being some playboy's latest conquest. She immediately reprimanded herself for being silly – she had no indication he wanted anything other than to be neighborly. Just because she couldn't stop mentally undressing the man didn't mean he had ulterior motives.

Jane told herself her mere attraction to Devon was a good sign; it meant the wounds left by Sam were finally beginning to heal. For the first time in a very long time, Jane allowed her mind to wander back to the time when she still believed in happily ever after.

Back then, she'd been convinced she loved him. She'd been elated about the possibilities stretched before them. Both of their families heartily approved of the engagement. It felt like the whole town celebrated with them when Sam finally proposed.

A sad smile played upon her lips as she remembered how earnest he'd looked, down on one knee at the church hayride. His sandy blond hair was a tousled mess; his bright blue eyes shone with excitement.

Jane angrily brushed away the single tear that slid its way down her cheek. She didn't want to think about Sam, and she certainly didn't want to spend her night sifting through the onslaught of emotions his memory would conjure. Mentally closing a door on the subject, she said a prayer for peace and willed her mind clear so the remnants of sangria could carry her off to sleep.

Instead of the blissful quiet she'd been hoping for, Jane's night was fitful at best. The images scrolling through her subconscious were filled with a confusing mix of desire and fear. Like an out-of-sync movie montage, one moment she was dreaming of doing delightful things to Devon McAlister, only to have the image fade into a nightmare with her being chased by an unknown, unseen evil.

When Jane's eyes finally popped open, she was surrounded by an eerie silence. The usual sounds of the jungle had stilled. She sensed that dawn was close, yet still far enough away she should try to find sleep again. But the silence wouldn't let her. After a few futile minutes of trying to recapture one of the happier dreams, she finally gave up and slid out of bed.

Jane pulled her mud boots on and grabbed her journal, wondering if the silence meant Deifilia had finally calmed down. As she stepped out of her cabin, it took a full moment for her brain to process that the jaguar's cage stood wide open. Her heart stopped. She opened her mouth to scream for the Guerreros, but the sound was cut short by a searing pain on the back of her head. Everything went black as she crumbled to the ground.

CHAPTER FIVE

EDUARDO DIDN'T WANT TO DO IT. As he watched her fall, he felt bad for hurting the pretty blonde. He paused for a moment to watch her prone form on the dirt, to assure himself she was still breathing.

He'd only come to let the jaguars out. Loose, they stood a chance. In their cages, they would surely die or be taken as prizes for Javier's collection. The deserved neither fate.

He'd watched the man leave before breaking the lock on the cage. He hadn't expected the American to come out of her cabin when she had. His plan had been to smoke the women out after he was well on his way back to Javier Barrera's compound. If anyone found out he'd been here, it would undoubtedly be a death sentence.

Movement in the house told him he hadn't silenced her in time. The other woman would soon be coming to investigate. He waited for her by the door. She never saw it coming.

His heart hammered in his throat as he took care of the women. Sweat dripped from him. He worried he'd throw up before it was done.

He didn't know where to go from there, what to do next. To go back home meant the risk of being found out. But with no money in his pocket, his chances of escaping to find a fresh start were less than slim.

Had he only to contend with Javier Barrera, Eduardo might have been willing to try running away from the jungle he called home.

But for years, there had been a much darker force pulling the drug lord's strings. It was a force that terrified Eduardo. He had no idea how vast its reach might be, but he did know it was great.

So he did the only thing he could think to do: He melted into the jungle.

CHAPTER SIX

JANE'S EYES FLUTTERED OPEN but were assaulted by sunlight, so she squeezed them shut again. Her head was throbbing. She tried to remember what was going on, why she was lying in the morning mist, why everything hurt. She slowly opened her eyes again as she gingerly pushed herself off the ground. The world spun as if she were on a tilt-a-whirl.

With both hands planted firmly on a tree stump for support, Jane paused to allow the earth beneath her to stop spinning. As it did, she began to register other sensations, like the acrid smell of smoke and the sound of Maria crying. She vaguely recalled stepping out of her cabin but had no clue why she was now lying in the underbrush between her cabin and the jungle.

It took every ounce of willpower Jane had to not curl up into the fetal position and simply wish it all away. With a deep breath, she pushed herself into the upright position. Once she was pretty sure the slightest movement wouldn't land her back on the dirt, she tentatively reached up to feel the source of the throbbing on the back of her head. It was warm and sticky. Jane pulled her hand away to stare at the blood covering it, struggling to make sense of what was going on.

"*Alabado sea Dios*! You're alive." Maria sprinted across the yard to Jane, who was still trying to survey the damage without falling down. The once-neat little compound now looked like a war zone.

Both houses had been reduced to smoldering piles of rubble and ash. The vet clinic stood in little better shape.

"Are you okay?" Jane gratefully accepted the woman's hug. "Where is Aldo?"

"I don't know, really. I just woke up, too. Aldo's not here. He got a call before dawn. One of the rangers found a hole in the perimeter fence, so he went to help fix it."

"Thank God." Jane breathed a sigh of relief. At least nobody had been seriously injured in the attack. "Somebody opened Deifilia's cage. I noticed it before I got hit on the head."

"Who hit us?"

"I didn't see. I just came outside and noticed the gate was open, and then everything went black."

"I can't believe they would do this to us. These people are our neighbors. I thought they were our friends."

Jane shook her head, instantly regretting the action. "I can't either. I knew the locals weren't crazy about the jaguar population going up, but I had no idea they were this determined to stop us."

"What do we do now?"

"I'm going to walk Deifilia's enclosure. Maybe she's still there, or at least the cubs are. You know how good she is at hiding them when she wants to."

"I'll help," Maria offered.

Out of the corner of her eye, Jane saw her journal lying neatly beside where she had been. The ground had never felt so far away as it did when she knelt down to pick it up, but somehow she managed. With her book tucked safely under her arm, she followed Maria.

Together the women combed every inch of the large enclosure. Jane would have felt marginally better about the entire process if she'd had a tranq gun with her, but she hadn't been able to find one, and with the cage open there was no guarantee they were any safer outside of it than in.

When their search turned up nothing, Jane admitted defeat with a heavy heart. "Let Aldo know Deifilia and her cubs are gone. I'll see if I can track them in the meantime."

"I'll start cleaning up, I guess." Maria gestured helplessly at the shambles that had once been their home.

"I don't like the thought of you being here alone," Jane protested.

"I'll call my sister. Her family will help."

"Okay, but be careful."

"You too."

The two women parted ways, each to her respective task. Jane looked back at her cabin, or what used to be her cabin. She held little hope of finding anything usable in there. But the vet clinic, it might still have something she could use as protection in the jungle.

There, after several minutes of searching, she was able to find one of the handguns Aldo kept for emergencies. The country girl in her would have felt more comfortable with a shotgun resting in the crook of her arm, but this would have to do. She also found a backpack and a water bottle.

It took fifteen minutes more to find the receiver for Deifilia's tracking collar, but the reward was worth the delayed start. Without it, the cat would be impossible to find. With it, she'd be difficult to find.

Once her meager survival gear was put together, Jane pointed herself in the direction the cat had gone and started walking. Naturally, the path led to Devon McAlister's land. When she reached the fence that marked the boundary between the two, she still hadn't found the mother or cubs. The green blip on the receiver told her she'd have to scale the fence if she wanted to get her jaguars back. Jane could almost picture God giggling over the irony.

She bit her bottom lip and stared at the fence for a moment, mentally cursing the luck, before grabbing hold of the chain link and hoisting herself up. She landed on the other side with a thud, pain shooting through her still-tender head. She closed her eyes and gave herself a second to pray away the pain before resolutely trekking closer to the blinking green light on the screen.

She finally reached the spot of the blink, stepping out of the dense jungle and onto a beaten path with two ruts obviously worn out by the wheels of a vehicle. There was no cat. She looked all around the area, but every time she moved from the spot she'd been in, the receiver indicated she was moving away from the transmitter. She went back to the spot where the jaguar was supposed to be and stood there, wondering what to do next.

Despite the dense vegetation on either side of the path, Jane saw no reason why she shouldn't be able to see the cat – especially since the receiver said she was standing in the exact spot. Jane scanned the trees again, and that's when she saw the transmitter hanging from a branch directly above her head.

"Damn it!" she shouted, her frustration reaching its boiling point. If her head didn't hurt so badly, she would have jumped up and down in a good old-fashioned temper tantrum. "Damn, damn, damn."

She sat down right in the middle of the path, only briefly trying to stem back the tears before deciding they were probably more helpful than letting loose a string of swear words that didn't feel right coming from her lips. She didn't know how long she sat there crying before she heard the rumble of a car drawing near.

The Jeep rolled to a stop in front of Jane before her foggy brain could register that she should get out of the way. Jane looked up into the smiling eyes of Devon McAlister and wondered if she was relieved or horrified.

One look at her tear-soaked face and his smile quickly faded. He was at her side before she could even form a hello.

"Are you okay?" Concern was etched on his brow as he knelt beside her.

"I'm fine." She tried to wave him off, but he was insistent on looking her over.

"You're not fine. You have a huge gash on the back of your head." He gently felt around the edges of the wound.

"If that's your definition of huge, you must have a trail of disappointed ladies in your wake." Jane couldn't resist the barb.

"I'm going to tell myself that's your head injury talking." Devon wrapped an arm around her waist and lifted Jane to her feet with such ease it made her feel like a ragdoll.

"Whatever makes you feel better, sweetie."

"You're mean when you're injured. Has anybody ever told you that?"

"I do believe I have heard that before," Jane admitted a little ruefully before adding with a measure of contrition, "I'll do my best to stop teasing you."

"Where would be the fun in that?"

Jane's brain was too muddled to come up with a witty reply, so she gave him an awkward smile instead. As she looked up at him, it occurred to her that his eyes were the prettiest shade of brown she'd ever seen. She wondered if there was such a thing as smoky brown. If so, that's what color his eyes were.

"I don't need any help." She attempted to put some distance between them.

"Then what are you doing on the road to my house with a huge— or rather, modest-sized—gash in your head?" Before she could answer, he amended his question with, "Don't get me wrong – I was delighted to find you here. I'm just curious."

"I'm looking for a jaguar, or rather, three of them."

"You know, when I was a kid, our neighbor's Doberman got loose once. I thought that was unnerving. I realize now it could have been worse."

"We were attacked last night; I'm still not sure what all went on, but whoever gave me the injury of disputed size also opened an enclosure."

"So there are three loose now?"

"Well," Jane hesitated a split second. "There could actually be more than that. Deifilia was the only jaguar wearing a radio collar, so I came looking for her and her cubs. But if she somehow managed to find her way here, there might be a hole in our fence line. I can't promise none of the other cats have found it."

"Ah."

"The receiver led me here." Jane pointed up. "But apparently it was for nothing."

He looked up, silently studying the transmitter hanging from the tree before he spoke. "Do you think she could have gotten the collar off by herself?"

"I highly doubt it. From here, it looks like someone took the collar off her."

"Any idea where the cubs might be?"

Jane shook her head, tears brimming in her eyes anew. Fear clenched her stomach as she thought of everything that could possibly happen to the cubs, Aria and Freya, if they were alone.

"Okay, here's what I think we should do: I'll call a friend who has bloodhounds so we can start tracking Deifilia and her cubs. While we're waiting for them to get here, we'll get Cass to stitch up your head."

"Who is Cass?"

"My assistant, Cassandra. My lifeline might be a better way to describe her."

"And your assistant knows how to stitch up a person's head?"

"In a pinch."

"How reassuring."

"I'm sure it'll be easy enough once she gets you shaved."

"Excuse me?"

Devon's lip curled into a mischievous smile in response. "Come on, let's get going. Leave the collar there so we know where to start our search."

"My head's really okay. I could start looking now and you can just join me when you're ready." Jane dug her heels in when Devon tried to lead her to the car.

"Cass won't really shave your head," he promised.

"Don't patronize me. I just want to keep looking."

"Are you always this stubborn?" He raised an eyebrow and pinned her with his gaze.

"Usually."

"Why won't you let me help you?"

"I'm just worried about Aria and Freya. The longer they're alone, the less chance I find them alive." While true, she was also beginning to worry about how easy it would be to let Devon step in and be a knight in shining armor. She had no intention of being anybody's damsel in distress.

"You aren't going to last long wandering around the jungle all by yourself with a concussion. Get in the Jeep," he ordered, adding after a pause a much gentler, "Please."

Jane realized in that moment he wasn't going anywhere without her, and she needed the bloodhounds he had access to if she had any hope of finding the jaguars. Grudgingly, she climbed into the passenger seat of the Jeep.

"Are you sure you don't have something better to be doing today?" Jane protested one last time as he put the car in gear. "Where were you headed to begin with?"

"I was driving out to see who or what tripped our perimeter alarm."

"So I tripped your alarm?"

He nodded in response.

"Did your alarm go off earlier, too? Before dawn, I mean."

"No, just this once."

"How's that possible?"

"Good question."

It was the question that hung in the air for the rest of the ride back to Devon's hacienda. When his home came into view, Jane couldn't help the way her breath caught. It was magnificent. The white Spanish-style home with blue trim, a rounded tile roof and stone chimney was lovely, but it was the vibrantly colored flowers in every hue that took her breath away. They trailed down the sides of the house and wound their way around the concrete pillars of the patio. Terracotta pots with more brightly colored flowers lined the patio. Tropical trees offered their branches for shade. Even from the driveway, Jane could hear the happy gurgle of water coming from the fountain that stood as his garden's centerpiece.

"Why do your roses smell so amazing?" Jane couldn't help blurting as she stepped out of the Jeep. "I thought commercial roses weren't supposed to have a scent."

"I'd rather cut production numbers and produce something that will bring people joy."

He seemed sincere, but Jane couldn't quite bring herself to believe him. "You're good. Very smooth."

"Don't ask questions if you aren't going to believe the answer," he admonished with a hint of amusement in his voice.

"You're serious?" She didn't know why she was struggling so much to take him at his word. She just was.

Laughter rumbled deep in his chest, which did nothing to convince her he meant what he said. The more she saw of his home, the more she felt sorry for the women who became ensnared in his web. It was gorgeous, perfectly put together, and had an open, appealing air to it. It was a happy place. It also left little doubt just how wealthy Devon was. Jane had always adored the little saltbox-style farmhouse she'd grown up in, but she had to admit it was a shack compared to the home she was now standing in. She wondered how many impoverished women succumbed to Devon in hopes of winning his pocketbook as well as his bed.

"If you go upstairs, down the hall and to the right, you'll find a bedroom with some clothes about your size in it. There's a bathroom in there you can use to clean up a bit if you'd like. I'll go find Cass."

"Do I want to know why you have women's clothes on hand?"

"I told you I have a sister. She used to visit more before she got married, though she is bringing her family down for a visit soon. She promised she would, anyway. Her adopted daughter is a princess, so plans have a way of changing at the last minute with them."

"She's that spoiled?" Jane frowned, unable to fathom her own mother ever changing plans for her.

"No, she's an actual princess," Devon clarified. "It's kind of a long story."

"I'd be curious to hear it sometime." Jane was embarrassed by her assumption. "And I appreciate the offer, but I don't need to clean up. I want to move quickly."

"You might want to make the time," he suggested with the hint of a knowing grin.

"Are you saying I smell bad?"

"No, I just think those of us helping you will have an easier time concentrating if you aren't in that camisole. Well, if you're in something more substantial than the camisole – because I have to be honest, all I can think about right now is you not in that camisole."

Jane's jaw dropped. She debated reprimanding him but couldn't begin to form the words.

"I was just being honest. I'm trying really hard to be a concerned gentleman, but it's damn near impossible at the moment."

"You're incorrigible" was the retort Jane finally settled on. If she was being honest, she would have admitted that she was at least the smallest bit pleased at his reaction to her. Even if he was just playing her, it was kind of nice to feel like an attractive woman.

"You don't believe me, do you? If we weren't pressed for time, I'd prove it."

Jane's breath quickened. For a split second, she considered rearranging her schedule, though she had zero intention of letting him know that. "I'll go get that shower now."

Devon's smile broadened and he nodded briefly before striding off to find his assistant and make the necessary phone calls.

Jane found the room he directed her to. Its walls were a pale yellow, adorned with stretched canvas prints of poppies in reds, oranges and yellows. In the closet, Jane found a wide array of clothes – everything from sundresses to jeans and T-shirts. Cute strappy heels sat virtually untouched, while the hiking boots looked like they'd been worn nearly bare. Jane decided Devon's sister was probably someone she could get along well with. She grabbed some jeans, a T-shirt, and the hiking boots then went to clean up.

As the water poured over her, all the adrenaline that had been propping her up began to ebb away, and Jane felt every ache and pain. Her head pounded anew. The reality of the morning settled in. Her home was destroyed. Her favorite jaguars were missing. She had no idea what had happened or why they'd been attacked.

And it seemed the person in the best position to help her find her jaguars was the one man who posed the greatest threat to her hard-won peace.

CHAPTER SEVEN

"YOU'RE SMILING LIKE A TOTAL FOOL."

"Am I?" Devon stopped scrolling through his contacts list long enough to look Cass Allen in the eye. "Do only fools smile, my darling Cassandra?"

"Only fools smile like that," she countered, neatly folding her arms across her chest as she managed to look down her nose at him despite the fact that there was more than a foot difference in their height.

"I suppose I'm happy," he mused.

"Happy that there are man-eating jaguars loose on your property, or that you get to spend the day searching for them instead of reading the summary from the last McAlister board meeting?"

"Happy for an excuse to spend more time with such a delightfully complex woman."

"It's always a woman."

"Not like this."

Cass's expression said she wasn't buying it. "I'll sew her head back together, but then I think you need to get your head back into work."

"You are a regular little ray of sunshine this morning, love."

"A ray of sunshine you would be lost without," she reminded him.

"Too true," he agreed, sighing in exasperation when he tapped the wrong name on the phone. "Stupid fat fingers. I hate this phone."

"That's your third phone this year. It's not the phone."

"You're rather unpleasant today. Do you realize that?"

"You've mentioned it. One day," she conceded. "Give yourself one day to find her jaguars and delight in her complexities, but then forget about the girl and remember how many families are depending on you."

"You don't fight fair."

"And it's one of the many things you love about me," she reminded him.

He looked up from his phone to acknowledge the truth in what she said before returning his attention to finding the phone number he was looking for. Cass let herself out of the office. As dear a friend as she was, he was glad to see her disapproval go with her.

Devon couldn't explain why, but he had an overwhelming desire to be the one to step in and save the day for Jane. It was absurd how badly he wanted to fix things for her. If he were in a reflective mood, he might have stopped to think about why that was, but he wasn't inclined to dwell on it at the moment.

It took him half an hour, but he was pleased to have good news for Jane. A search party with bloodhounds was loading up at that very moment to head their way. There was a spring in his step when he set out to find her.

He'd told himself he'd be able to focus better once Jane was properly dressed. Once he saw her, he realized he'd been happily wrong. Even in jeans and a T-shirt, she still looked amazing. The faded blue denim and buttery soft material of the washed out shirt clung to her curves invitingly. She looked like a present waiting to be unwrapped. Her blond curls had been pulled loosely into a ponytail at the base of her head; tendrils were already escaping their bounds. His fingers itched to touch one of them.

"Good news," she informed him without emotion. "No stitches. Cass says the cut isn't deep."

"That's excellent." He wondered why she'd passed up the opportunity to tease him about his ability to ascertain size. "I have news too. The search party will be here any minute; then we can all head over together."

"Wonderful. Thank you." She seemed sincere but reserved. Devon looked from Jane to Cass. He didn't have to wonder too hard what had happened.

When Jane excused herself to call Aldo, Devon turned to find out exactly what Cass had said to her, but the woman had disappeared without a word, leaving him all alone with his irritation. Cass had never bothered to keep him away from anyone before. When he got a chance, he was going to have to chat with her about just where their boundary lines were.

Jane's expression when she rejoined him in the office made Devon stop short. Her ashen pallor and tear-filled eyes were all he needed to see before striding across the room to envelop her in a hug.

"What's wrong? What happened?"

To Devon, it seemed like an eternity that her only response was silent tears. She didn't fight his embrace; rather she melted into his arms, burying her face against his chest. Finally, her answer came barely above a whisper. "Aldo called. They found Deifilia. She's been killed."

"Oh, Jane. I'm so sorry." He didn't know what else to say, what else to do. It was one of those helpless moments when all the wealth and charisma in the world weren't doing him a bit of good. He hated those moments.

He didn't ask how or why; it wasn't the time for whys. Now was the time to simply be there for her. So he held her close, stroked her hair, and wished like hell he could do more.

"Her body wasn't far from my cabin."

"So somebody moved the collar onto my land," Devon surmised.

The fact that it was done without tripping the alarms hung in the air between them.

"Why would someone do that?" Jane looked up at him.

"To get you to follow the transmitter, although I'm not sure why."

"We have to find those cubs – now more than ever." She slowly pushed away from Devon and wiped her eyes. Her quiet strength made him want to pull her close again.

Instead of hiding her in his embrace, he resolved to find those cubs for her, no matter what. "Absolutely. Come on; the hounds will be here any moment. Now that we know the collar was a decoy, we'll start where they found Deifilia."

Leading people was something he could do, so for the next several hours, he threw all he had into organizing the locals who'd shown up to help search. Even though it was determined the fences were down in three places, none of the adult jaguars had left their territory. But as evening drew near, the cubs hadn't been found.

Devon tried unsuccessfully to get Jane to stop for lunch. By dinner, he was insistent. "You haven't eaten all day. You've got a head injury. If you push yourself much harder, you're going to collapse."

"I don't collapse," Jane stanchly informed him, stubbornly refusing to stop.

Devon sighed as she veered down another path. "You've never once conceded that something was beyond your control, have you?"

"That's not true," she countered. "But I'm not conceding this."

"I'll make you a deal." He took her by the shoulders and turned her to face him. "One of my friends is heading home for the evening. I trust him completely. Why don't you hitch a ride with them back to my house? Have some dinner and get a nice long bath, then go to sleep. I promise I won't come home until either I've found the kittens or you've rejoined me."

"I can't sleep and just expect you to fix this for me," she protested.

"And I don't have the first idea what to do with two three-week-old jaguars if I find them. You need to be rested and able to take care of them." He could sense she was yielding. "I promise I won't get a big head about it or anything if I find them."

"Somehow I doubt you'll be able to keep that promise."

"You have no faith in me at all, do you?" He was unable to keep the exasperation out of his voice.

She gave him a look filled with startling honesty. "You're probably right; I seem to have lost my faith in most of mankind."

He wanted to ask her who had stolen that from her but knew now was not the time. "I'll do everything in my power to help you reclaim it, then."

Her eyes searched his in the fading light of day. For the first time in a very long time, he feared he would be found wanting, that she would peer deep into his soul and reject what she saw there. After an excruciating silence, she nodded slightly. "Okay. I'll eat and get some rest."

"Thank you." He breathed a sigh of relief. It was crazy how happy her trust made him. Once he had her safely loaded in the cab of Pablo's pickup truck, Devon renewed his search with zeal.

The cliché "needle in a haystack" came to mind as night closed in. Just ahead of him, one of Luis Perez's bloodhounds happily jogged down a trail forged by his nose. At this stage of the game, all of their hopes were pinned on a slobbering beast with jowls too big for his face. Devon had little choice but to keep following the dog and his trainer.

Now that they were completely enveloped in darkness, Devon was keenly aware they were on a jaguar preserve. He recalled hearing once that the name jaguar meant "he who kills with one leap," and that led him to wonder just how many of the animals roamed the jungle he currently scoured.

One of the bloodhounds to their left began baying, his distinctive bawl signaling he smelled something. Devon and his search partner looked at each other hopefully before taking off in the direction of the commotion.

It didn't take long for their dog to pick up on the same scent. His heart raced with excitement as a third dog joined the chorus. They had to be close to something.

"Here!" someone shouted. Devon made his way over to the craggy tree where Luis knelt, pointing at the two hissing cubs. Though they tried their best to appear menacing, Devon thought their protests were ridiculously cute. He couldn't help the joy that bubbled into laughter. They'd actually found them. Several of the men who'd gathered looked at him like he'd lost his mind. Several others joined his laughter. He considered calling Jane to tell her, but there was a selfish piece of him that wanted to see the look on her face when she got the news.

The kittens were tucked back far enough that he almost couldn't reach them. It took a moment of fishing before he had both of them out. Luis called for a truck to come pick them up at the nearest road as Devon tucked the babies under his arms. He refused to let them out of his sight.

Once they were bumping along the dirt road back to his house, he called Aldo to tell him the good news and extend an invitation to the couple to stay with him until their home could be rebuilt. Then he called his head housekeeper to request a meal be prepared for the weary searchers.

"Lucia, is our guest resting?" he asked.

"She fell asleep after her bath. I took her some bread and cheese, but last I checked, it hadn't been touched."

"Thank you for trying."

When they got back to his house, he instructed the men to help themselves to anything they needed. After placing the search party in Lucia's capable care, he scooped the jaguar cubs into his arms again and headed straight for Jane's room. Once there, he debated how best to knock with his hands full. The cubs had stopped hissing at him, but once he stood outside Jane's room, they began a distinctive squeak that made him stop to really look at them for the first time in the light.

They looked back up at him unblinkingly with their still-blue eyes. Their disproportionately large heads bobbled slightly as they sized him up. It was the first time he thought about them, about what they'd been through, how close they'd come to death, or what their day had been like. Up until that moment, he'd been searching for them to make Jane happy. Something passed between man and animal in his upstairs hallway, though. He now understood Jane's fierce desire to protect them.

"You're okay now," he promised with a whisper before using his forehead to knock on Jane's door.

She opened it faster than he expected. He wondered if she'd been awoken by their arrival or if she hadn't been asleep after all. The look on her face was worth every moment he'd spent looking. She lit up from the inside out.

"My sweet babies!" she exclaimed, reaching out to take Aria from him. The kitten stopped mewing and made a sound that was much more like a purr.

"She knows you." Devon was incredulous. When the kitten in his arms squirmed, he instinctively handed her to Jane as well. Freya's own sound of contentment joined her sister's.

Jane's laughter was light and happy as she sank to the floor with both jaguar cubs. They climbed on her with their wobbly legs, licking her skin and making their odd little purr with each exhale.

Devon sat down on the floor with her, enraptured by the scene unfolding before him.

"They'll need to eat." Jane's smile faltered. "I'm not sure if our milk replacer made it through the fire."

"Aldo is on his way over. If he doesn't bring any with him, we have some fresh goat's milk that would probably be better than nothing."

"Thank you." Jane nodded. She hugged each of the cubs to her again before looking back to Devon. "I can't believe you found them. Thank you so much."

"I told you I was here if you ever needed anything." He couldn't tear his eyes away from her face. Her beauty was enchanting. There was a sparkle in her smile that made him obsessed with seeing it again.

"You did say that," she conceded. "I just didn't think you actually meant it."

He didn't remember inching closer to her, yet somehow he found her near enough to reach out and touch. Of its own accord, his hand reached out to brush her cheek tenderly with his fingertips. "I've surprised even myself with just how much I meant it."

"You are good," she accused yet again, breaking the spell of the moment by looking down at Freya.

Devon cleared his throat self-consciously. "I heard a vicious rumor that you never ate dinner."

"I couldn't."

"Lucia is making dinner for the entire search party. You should join us."

"Maybe after I feed them," she suggested.

"May I help?"

"I don't want to be rude to everyone who helped."

"They won't mind." Devon didn't actually care if they did. "Wait right here. I'll go see what I can find. I'll be right back."

While downstairs, he asked Lucia to prepare two plates for them upstairs. "Could you send up some of that sangria you made last week, too?" he added as an afterthought.

Lucia ducked her head, but not before Devon caught a glimpse of her grin.

"Where's Cass?" He realized with a start he hadn't seen his assistant since that morning. She hadn't checked in, either. It wasn't like her.

"She left shortly after you did, *señor*. She said she was taking the day off since you were."

"Ah. Thank you." He made a mental note to follow up with Cass the next day to see if there was something bothering her. He couldn't fathom why she was that upset over his interest in Jane.

"Aldo and Maria are here. They couldn't find their supplies, so I called my daughter and asked her to bring over a couple of her baby's bottles. I had Pablo set aside some of the evening's milk just in case we found them," Lucia informed him.

Devon kissed her soundly on the cheek. "You are fantastic. Pablo is lucky I don't woo you away from him."

Lucia merely shook her head and waved him away. "Go visit with your guests for a few minutes. I'll have everything sent up to the *señorita*'s room."

The search party had turned into a celebration. Weariness faded as wine poured freely and an abundance of food was placed before them. Devon directed the Guerreros to the room where Jane was while he spent a few moments mingling with his guests. As soon as he could reasonably excuse himself, he hurried back to her room as well, hoping he hadn't missed his chance to see her feed Aria and Freya.

When he entered her room, he felt as nervous as a schoolboy on his first date. He stood with one hand on the door, unsure if he was intruding on the friends.

"Devon, please come in," Jane invited warmly.

"They seem like they're none the worse for the wear," Devon commented, though his eyes never left Jane.

"They're doing well, thanks to you." Aldo came to stand by Devon, clapping him on the shoulder as he did.

"We can't thank you enough for stepping in," Maria agreed warmly. "If there's ever anything we can do to repay you, please let us know."

"No repayment needed." Devon meant it, too. He was receiving his reward at that very moment, watching Jane's hair fall across her shoulders as she tickled Aria's stomach.

"We appreciate you letting us stay here for the night," Maria added.

"My home is yours for as long as you need," he promised before turning his attention back to Jane. "Do you think the bottles Lucia sent up will work?"

"I was just getting ready to try them."

"If you two don't mind, we'll go eat with the others and let you feed the girls." Aldo motioned for his wife to join him. Devon appreciated the gesture, regardless of the lack of subtlety.

When they were alone, Jane smiled ruefully at Devon. "I'm sorry. They're determined to set me up with any single man in a twenty-mile radius."

"And here I thought I was special." He swiped the two bottles of goat's milk off the dresser and eased himself onto the floor beside her.

"Oh, I'm sure you are." She patronizingly patted his knee before taking one of the bottles from him.

"I'm going to tell myself you meant that." He watched how she fed one of the cubs before attempting to follow her lead. "This isn't as easy as it looks."

"They'll get the hang of it, and so will you."

His eyes drank in her every move. She was altogether lovely, the way she moved, the sound of her voice as she crooned lovingly at the little jaguar. As she smiled down at Aria with adoration in her eyes, he pictured her smiling down at a baby. It was just a flash of an image before he pulled himself back into the moment, before he reminded himself that he was a short-term kind of guy.

"I can't tell you how many hours I have spent over the past three weeks, watching Deifilia with these cubs. She was so gentle with them. She seemed to find contentment taking care of them. She was always so patient with them – grooming them while they rolled around batting at her and each other, being silly little kittens. I remember being so amazed at how she just knew what to do. No one told her; she just knew."

"One day, you'll be taking care of your own babies with that same natural instinct." He tried to shove aside the mental image that resurfaced.

"No, I won't." Sadness filled her eyes.

"You will, Janey. I'm sure of it."

"No, Devon, I won't. I can't have children."

CHAPTER EIGHT

JANE TRIED NOT TO DWELL ON IT too much, yet she couldn't help wondering what had come over her, why she'd blurted out something so personal to Devon. She'd seen pity in his eyes; she was sure of it. At least she hadn't seen repulsion – not that a man like him would care one way or another about her reproductive status.

She'd changed the subject after that, but the conversation had lost its earlier happy tone. Now she lay curled up in bed, snuggling her pillow and watching the jaguars sleep. The steady rise and fall of their bellies as they breathed brought her comfort.

Jane tried to think of something else. Unfortunately, the next thought to take its place was of Deifilia, followed closely by the damage done to Jane's home. Most of the day's search party had consisted of local farmers, so she would be really surprised if one of them had orchestrated the attack on the preserve. Jane understood they'd only been there as a favor to Devon, but she still couldn't picture any of them hitting two unarmed women over the head and then setting their homes on fire.

She couldn't fathom who else besides those farmers would gain from the ruination of the preserve, though. Even thinking about who could have killed Deifilia and moved her collar made her brain hurt. It made no sense whatsoever.

And then there was Cass. Jane didn't care if the woman was 90 pounds soaking wet; there was still something terrifying about her.

The little pit bull had warned Jane away from Devon in no uncertain terms. Jane had told her to save her breath, that she had zero interest in Devon McAlister, but Cass didn't believe it for a minute. Maybe Jane had stretched the numbers a bit when she'd said zero, but she still felt Cass's vehement warning had been unwarranted.

Jane didn't blame the woman, though. She could tell Devon was oblivious to it, but Jane was quite certain Cass's devotion to him ran deeper than employee loyalty. She knew it wasn't hers to judge, but in her opinion that was one of the problems with being a player: Someone always got hurt in the game, however unintentionally.

She reminded herself that Devon's love life, or rather sex life, was really none of her business. He'd proven himself to be a kind neighbor and maybe even someone she would one day call friend, but neither role gave her the right to analyze the depth of his life or lack thereof. It wasn't his fault he was charmed, and it certainly wasn't her place to determine the morality of his actions.

Jane said a little prayer for peace, but even as she whispered the words, she knew she didn't wholly mean them. On some level, she clung to the restlessness, fearing the emptiness that would take its place instead. She felt like she'd seen too much of life; she knew too much about the meanness people harbor in their hearts. Most days she kept it locked away and managed to function quite well. Some days the knowledge was brutally thrust into her face, and she was left feeling shell-shocked and laid bare.

Jane gave up on sleep and grabbed her journal, sitting up in bed and pulling her knees up to use her legs as a table. She began to recount the day in feminine scrawl. The act of putting pen to paper helped her sort out the jumble in her brain. As she tried recall the name of the man who'd given her a ride back to Devon's that evening, she came to the humbling realization that she'd been in this village for over a year and still didn't know the names of most of her neighbors. Had she really built a wall that high around her heart?

She also noticed something she'd completely missed before. The day might have started off with one terrible act, but the rest of it was filled with acts of kindness. These people, whom she'd always held at arm's length, came through for her today. Whether it was for her or for Devon didn't matter.

By the time she'd finished emptying the events of the day onto the pages of her book, she set aside the journal and flipped off the light, determined to get some sleep before the cubs needed to be fed again. Her last thoughts before drifting off were to wonder if she'd allowed her pain to change her into something she was never meant to be.

Her dreams that night were the weird kind, the ones where one minute she was standing in a grocery store shopping for eggs and the next she was a trapeze artist in the circus. The only scene from the whole night that made any sense to her at all also made her blush in the light of day. It also made her wonder if Devon was truly that skilled, or if her mind had begun to assign him superhuman qualities after the way he stepped in to save the day.

Jane's stomach rumbled, reminding her she'd once again missed a meal that had been laid before her. Now she was trembling with hunger, so she hurried through getting ready and kitten-proofing her room before setting out in search of food.

Determined to get facing Devon over with, just in case seeing him conjured memories of her dream that would cause her to blush again, Jane decided to pop her head into his office to say good morning. Then she could use her hunger as an excuse to bid a hasty retreat if necessary.

She held her hand up to tap on the partly opened door but was stopped short by his low growl. "Damn it, Cass!"

"I did it for your own good." The woman's response was close to a hiss. "You always think with your libido. Fine – bed her and get on with it. Just stop this foolishness. I need you here, doing your job."

Jane didn't need to hear any more. She tiptoed down the hallway, hoping like crazy she'd go unnoticed. The trembling in her hands was no longer from lack of sustenance. She didn't think she could eat now if her life depended on it; she was too nauseated.

Not knowing where else to go, she went to the kitchen anyway. If nothing else, it gave her somewhere to be without risking walking back by Devon's office.

"*Buenos días*! How are you on this lovely day? How are the babies?" Lucia greeted her warmly.

Jane did her best to smile back. "I'm well, thank you. Aria and Freya are wonderful. They appreciated the goat's milk, and the bottles worked great."

"I'll be sure to have them cleaned before the next feeding."

"You don't have to do that; I can."

"Nonsense, it's my job. I'm happy to do it. If you need me to step in for a feeding, I'd love the time with the babies," Lucia offered.

"I might take you up on that if I spend the day helping clean up over at the preserve."

"What can I make you for breakfast?"

"Some coffee would be divine."

Lucia poured Jane a cup of coffee, giving Jane a stern look. "And what will you have to eat?"

"I'm not hungry." Jane perched on one of the bar stools at the kitchen's immense island.

"When did you eat last?"

Jane hesitated before quietly yielding. "Some toast would be appreciated."

Lucia gave a barely perceptible nod before setting about Jane's breakfast. "You seem sad, *cariño*."

"I'm sorry." Jane took a sip of her coffee. "Oh my, that's amazing."

"You don't have to apologize for seeming sad. Do you want to talk about what's wrong?"

"I don't know what's wrong," Jane admitted. "I suppose I've just had a bit of a necessary reality check. Not that it should have been necessary. So I guess I've just been saved some heartache, and that's a good thing. It's silly to be sad."

Lucia regarded her silently, waiting for Jane's rambling to stop.

"I feel much better now; thank you."

"Glad to have helped." Lucia served Jane a plate of eggs, bacon and pancakes with a glass of juice.

"This is not toast. How did I not notice you making this?"

"You were busy working things out. No, it's not toast. It's one of *Señor* Devon's favorite meals, and I thought real food might do you some good. You were sounding a little crazed."

Jane had to admit she probably was sounding crazed, so she didn't bother to counter the woman's words. "Thank you. If it's even half as good as the coffee, I'm in for a real treat."

"Thank you." Lucia smiled and patted Jane's hand before moving off to dish up another plate. "A friend of mine grows the coffee. I've been serving it to *Señor* Devon in hopes of convincing him to branch out into fair trade coffee."

"Why are you trying to get him involved in coffee?"

"Because everything he touches flourishes, and it would be good for these people. His roses have changed their lives."

"Really?" Jane was intrigued.

"*Señor* Devon is a smart man with a good heart," Lucia pronounced. In that moment, Jane got the distinct impression that his aging housekeeper would throw down with anyone who dared suggest otherwise.

"Aw, now, you're making me blush." Devon's deep, smooth voice rumbled close to Jane, making her jump. Her fork clanged against the plate. She flushed with embarrassment and focused on straightening her place setting.

"I didn't hear you come in." She tried to sound nonchalant, but he was standing close enough now she could feel his presence, feel the heat radiating off of him. It was causing a new kind of heat to build from the pit of her belly, and that conjured images of last night's crazy trapeze dream, which only served to deepen her blush.

"I'm delighted to catch you ladies talking about me. It's all good, I hope." He eased himself onto the stool closest to Jane, despite there being two others to choose from.

Lucia bestowed an adoring smile on Devon and placed his breakfast in front of him.

"Lucia was just telling me how your rose plantation has bettered the lives of the locals. I was pleasantly surprised to hear it after some of the horrible reports I'd heard about the rose industry before moving here."

Devon's face darkened. "Unfortunately, those reports probably don't even scratch the surface. The industry as a whole is in a deplorable state. Work conditions are hellish, and the product being shipped overseas isn't even safe to be touched, let alone sit in a kitchen vase."

"That's horrible." Jane wondered if she'd ever stop being surprised to learn the depths her species was sinking to.

"But we run things differently here," he assured her. "If you have time to take a break from the clean-up effort, I'd be delighted to show you around sometime."

"I'd like that." Jane meant it. Touring his rose plantation sounded much more pleasant than sifting through the rubble of her broken dreams. She highly doubted she'd have the time in the near future, though.

"Good." He beamed at her before turning his attention to his breakfast.

Lucia disappeared, presumably off to set about her day's work. That left Jane with her thoughts, which vacillated between preoccupation with his nearness and remembrance of overhearing Devon's argument with the woman he'd just yesterday proclaimed to be his lifeline. Jane didn't know what to make of it. She was also irritated with herself for caring.

"Is your breakfast okay?"

She looked down at the plate of barely touched food. "It's wonderful. Thank you for your hospitality."

He eyed her speculatively but didn't say anything.

"I should probably go check on the babies."

"Pablo is preparing them a stall in the barn."

"The barn?" Jane was dismayed.

"I assumed your eventual goal would be to release them into the wild, or at least the preserve," he explained. "I can't imagine they'll fare well if they become housecats."

"You're right. I just hadn't thought that far ahead yet." It galled her to admit it.

"They'll have a turnout for plenty of sunshine and a safe, dry place, too," he promised.

"Thank you. I'm going to miss them, though."

"Then we'll just have to find other ways to occupy your time," he suggested.

"You're disgusting!" Jane knew she was overreacting, but Cass's advice to "bed her and get it over with" was still ringing in her ears, and that seemed to override any filters on Jane's brain.

"I meant dinner or something." He held his hands up defensively. "But if I had meant that, I don't think disgusting is the right adjective."

"We'll just have to agree to disagree on that one." Jane dropped her fork and pushed herself away from the island. "I've got to go find Aldo and Maria."

"They're already over at the preserve. Would you like a ride?"

"No, thank you." Her reply was clipped.

"Do you want to borrow a horse?"

"I don't ride."

"Are you going to scale my fence again, then? Because it's too long of a walk on the road, and it's not necessarily safe until we know who attacked the preserve."

Not wanting to seem petulant, Jane fought the urge to glare at him. "I suppose I will have to accept that ride, after all."

"I promise not to steal your virtue on the way there." His tone was uncharacteristically terse.

"You wouldn't recognize virtue if it walked up and bit you on the ass."

"Neither would you," he tossed back before curtly instructing her, "Be ready in five minutes."

"Thank you," she snapped before storming out of the kitchen, nearly bumping into Cass on her way out the door. Part of Jane wanted to verbally eviscerate the woman right then and there because it would go a long way toward relieving her frustrations, but she reminded herself she was a guest in this home and nowhere in the Bible did Jesus tell her to verbally annihilate her enemies. With those two facts reining her temper, she simply muttered a feeble "Excuse me" before running up the stairs to round up the jaguar cubs.

It was closer to ten minutes later when Devon came to retrieve her from the stables. Aria and Freya were sprawled in the straw, batting at each other's faces with uncoordinated paws. He gave Jane a minute to rattle off last-minute instructions and thanks to Pablo before reminding her he had to leave.

"Do you have a big day planned? You seem to be in a hurry," Jane asked once they were on their way, attempting to keep her voice pleasant.

"I have a house full of company arriving over the next several days and some really important paperwork to finish before they get here," he responded, his tone carrying the same forced politeness as hers.

"Oh, we can leave, then. I don't mean to be in your way." Jane suddenly felt guilt-ridden for so completely disrupting his life.

"And go where?" he posed.

Jane's response was delayed. "That's not your problem, Devon. Nobody is going to think you're a bad guy for not wanting your neighbors to move in on you."

"How is it any less my problem than anybody else's? If I don't help you, who will? I truly don't mind, Jane. Stop being so stubborn."

"That's like asking me to stop breathing," she quipped, then quietly regarded him for a moment. His words now seemed so incongruous with his shallow playboy reputation. "I don't know what to make of you sometimes."

"I never know what to make of you." He put the car into park in front of what used to be her cabin and turned to face her. They sat there in silence, just watching each other, and for that moment time suspended.

She had to admit he was a beautiful man, the very definition of tall, dark, and handsome. Her fingers itched to find their way in into his dark, tousled hair. A layer of perpetual scruff nearly concealed his dimple when he smiled at her. There was something about that smile that made her want to sink into him. She wondered what it would be like to be pressed against his defined muscles, to feel his strong arms wrapped tightly around her. She wondered what his lips tasted like.

Her body's visceral reaction to him was exactly why she knew she should get herself out of that car, fast. It was a really good reason to live in a tent on the preserve instead of in a room right down the hall from his.

"Why?" Jane realized with horror that she'd uttered the question aloud.

"Why what?" Devon shifted to lean closer, his voice soft and gentle.

She wanted to shout, "Why you? Why now?" Her body had chosen the most inconvenient moment and person possible to react to. Stupid pheromones. Instead of posing the questions she knew he couldn't answer, she merely shook her head. "Nothing. It's stupid. Thank you for the ride."

When she would have hopped out of the car, Devon leaned over her and pulled the door closed.

"Devon, I can't do this right now," she protested.

Still leaning across her, he placed a finger on her lips. She saw the warning in his eyes and froze. That's when she heard the voices and noticed the truck that didn't belong to Aldo and Maria, or anyone else she knew. She opened her mouth to offer the hopeful suggestion that maybe it belonged to someone Aldo had called in to help rebuild, when two men emerged from the jungle with automatic rifles slung on their backs.

Devon's reaction was swift; he threw his Jeep into gear and sped back down the driveway. Instinctively, Jane reached for the phone on his hip. He seemed to know what she wanted and shifted positions so she could unholster it.

She breathed a sigh of relief when Aldo answered the phone, seemingly unconcerned.

"Where are you?" She watched as Devon flew past his own driveway. A glance in the rearview mirror told her why. The other truck was closing in.

"We stopped by Luis's to return a flashlight and wound up staying for breakfast. What's wrong, *mi hija*?"

"There were men with guns at the preserve. They're chasing us now. Don't go back there until we figure out what's going on." Jane didn't know if she was making any sense.

"There are men chasing you with guns?"

"Yeah, kind of. Yes. We'll be fine. Just stay in touch and stay away from the preserve."

"What can we do? Where are you?"

"I'm with Devon. It'll be okay. Just keep yourself safe. That's all I need." She tried to hang up the smartphone, but it wasn't responding to her swipe. She muttered "stupid phone" and tried one last time, finally triumphing.

"Ha! It *is* the phone." Devon shifted his hips again so she could slide it back in its holster. "Hang on."

Jane braced her hands on the dash, but Devon's hard left turn still jolted her.

"Where are you going?"

"Are you up for being on foot for a bit? I know a back way in."

Jane nodded but secretly wished she'd had breakfast after all. It was starting to hit her full force that she hadn't eaten in 48 hours, and it had been a crazy couple of days to boot.

"Good. When I stop, hit the ground running. We're heading north. Stay close."

She nodded again and glanced in the mirror. Devon had pulled ahead enough to buy them the time they needed to disappear into the jungle. The instant the Jeep stopped, she jumped out and ran for all she was worth. Even so, she struggled to keep up with Devon's long strides. High school track felt like a lifetime ago, as evidenced by the burning in her lungs.

Tree limbs smacked her in the face. Thorns and underbrush clawed at her skin and clothes. Her legs screamed from the exertion. Still she pressed on, keeping Devon well in sight. When she burst out of the trees into a clearing, he reached out and grabbed hold of her, pulling Jane to him just before she ran straight off the edge of a cliff.

"Oh, dear Lord," she gasped, clinging to his shoulders and burying her face against his chest. His heart was hammering as hard as hers. The thunder of a waterfall filled her ears. She couldn't hear anything else; she had no way of knowing if their pursuers were still behind them.

"I think we should jump."

"I think you're crazy."

"Probably, but I still think we should jump," he persisted.

Jane peeked over the edge. The water seemed pretty darn far below to her. "Holy crap. I still think you're crazy."

He spun her back around and cupped her chin in his hands. "Trust me, Janey. Please."

She paused for a beat, searching his eyes. "Okay. On three?"

Their pursuers were closer now; Jane could hear them above the roar of water.

"Three." Devon grabbed her hand and pulled her with him over the edge of the cliff.

CHAPTER NINE

THE FREEFALL TO WATER lasted just long enough for Devon to wonder if he'd killed them both – and to think he liked the way her hand felt in his, even as they plummeted through the air. The crash into the water knocked the wind out of him, but he was happy to be alive—and happier still when he felt Jane struggling to resurface.

They popped out of the water, sputtering for air. Without a word, Devon tucked Jane to his side and kicked his strong legs, propelling them to shore. He'd lived in the basin long enough to know they hadn't survived the jump yet, not until they were out of reach of the myriad of predators who called this river home.

Their pursuers fired at them in vain. Devon wasn't sure whether it was divine providence or the fact that the distance was too great for the bullets to find their target, but he wasn't willing to stick around to see if their luck would hold. The pair crawled out of the water, still gasping for air, and stumbled into the protection of the jungle.

Devon cast a worried glance at Jane when she stopped to lean against a nearby tree with her eyes closed. "Do you have a little bit more in you?"

"Yeah, I'm fine." She shoved away from the tree. "Just point me where you want me to go, boss."

"Are you sure?"

She replied with a look that adequately conveyed her irritation.

"Okay then." He took her by the shoulders and turned her to face north. "That way."

Devon knew he needed to take the lead since he was the one who knew where they were going, but he was loath to let Jane out of his field of vision. She looked pale and shaky. And tired.

As they trudged through the dense vegetation, Devon wondered what kind of trouble his pretty little neighbor had landed herself in the middle of. Neither spoke much; they were both too tired and unsettled.

When Devon finally broke the silence, it was to let her know they didn't have much farther to go before reaching a cabin where they could take a break and get a drink of water. "Can you make it a little longer?"

"Would you stop asking me that? It's patronizing."

"How is concern for your welfare patronizing?" He stopped and turned to her. "You look like you could collapse at any moment."

"I told you before, I don't collapse."

Those were the last words to leave her mouth before she crumpled like an old marionette at his feet. He felt a little bad for not catching her, but it had taken him by such surprise he hadn't reacted quickly enough. Jane had been so adamant about not collapsing, he'd believed her.

"Well, this sucks," he told no one in particular before kneeling to scoop her unconscious form into his arms. She wasn't a large woman and he considered himself to generally be a strong man, but the added weight made his already tired muscles protest. Suddenly the cabin felt much farther away than it had five minutes ago – not that he'd ever tell Jane that. Of course, it was probably best if he didn't tell her he hadn't caught her, either.

Devon resolutely set out toward the cabin. By the time the building came into view, he was happier to see it than he ever had been before. Once there, he laid her on the bed and gently tugged her wet boots and socks off. Then he hesitated. If it were anyone else in the world, he'd strip them down to their skivvies and put a warm blanket around them.

But this was Jane, and that posed a whole new set of problems. For one, he wasn't entirely sure he wanted the first time he saw her in her underwear to be while she was unconscious. That just seemed too creepy. For another, there was a very distinct possibility she would be really pissed at him if she woke up in her underwear.

Still, she looked miserable in her soaked clothes. He reminded himself he was a grown man and the head of several corporations. Surely he could be adult about helping a friend in need and weather any fallout from that decision.

"Okay then," he told himself aloud, feeling a little silly as he reached down to tug her T-shirt up. It was an awkward process, disrobing a woman who was completely passed out. This certainly wasn't how he'd been envisioning undressing her for the past several days. He was fairly proud of himself by the time he finally had Jane's clothes in a sopping heap on the floor and a warm blanket tucked around her.

He looked down at her on the bed; she looked so fragile. He couldn't resist reaching down to brush aside the blond ringlets that clung to her cheek. Then he surprised himself by leaning over and kissing her tenderly on the forehead. She murmured in response. He froze, wondering if he'd been caught in his impetuous gesture of affection. She sighed and settled deeper into her pillow.

He straightened and took a step back. He didn't understand what it was about her that brought about such a tumult of unfamiliar emotions. It irritated him not being able to sort it all out. Absolutely, she was beautiful, but he was accustomed to beautiful women. What magic power did she have that held him so captive? Was it her apathy – was he truly that shallow?

Thunder rumbled in the distance, telling him they would be waiting out a storm in the little cabin. He scowled. That's just what he needed, to be confined in a small space with a stunning, nearly naked woman he couldn't touch.

Devon unbuttoned his own shirt and hung it over a chair back. He glanced back at Jane to determine just how asleep she was before kicking off his jeans as well. He realized there was a small chance their pursuers had picked up their trail and would stumble across him in his boxers, but he kind of figured they wouldn't have bothered jumping off a cliff for the chase. Besides, wet jeans were a miserable enough experience that he was willing to take the risk.

Once the clothing dilemma was solved, Devon began rooting through the cabinets to see what supplies were still there. He found a bag of rice, so he poured some in a bowl and tossed his phone in it. The odds of wicking away enough water to make the phone work again were slim, but it was worth a shot. It wasn't an unmanageable walk back to the main house from where they were, but he imagined everyone would be worried about them long before they made it there. He'd love to be able to call home to reassure someone they were okay.

With the phone taken care of, he made them some lunch. It wasn't much—fresh fruit, plain rice, and beef jerky—but it was sustenance. At the moment, he was desperate to get some form of nutrition into Jane. The more he thought about it, the more certain he was she'd not eaten since before this whole mess began.

When he had a plate ready for her, he went to kneel beside the bed, stroking her cheek with the back of his free hand. "Janey, honey, wake up."

Her eyelids fluttered open; confusion clouded her sweet face.

"I have some food for you. You need to eat. You collapsed," he explained.

"I don't collapse."

"Then you chose a very inconvenient time for a nap. Either way, I have your lunch ready."

"Where are we?" Jane struggled to sit up, gasping in horror when the blanket fell to her lap and she realized her shirt was gone. She yanked the cover back to her. Her eyes flew to Devon. "Where are my clothes? Where are *your* clothes?"

"We're in a cottage on my property, not too terribly far from the main house. We can start walking that way once the storm passes and when you feel up to it. Our clothes are hanging up to dry in the meantime. Not exactly how I intended to get you naked, I admit." Devon winked at her and gave her an easy smile.

Jane hit him upside the head with her pillow, sending beef jerky and passion fruit skittering across the floor. "You ass! Who says you were ever going to get me naked to begin with?"

There was a shriek to her voice that gave Devon the distinct impression she was not amused by his charm.

The pillow hit him across the head again and he jumped back. She was up on her knees now in a full-on pillow assault. "Just because that scary little sidekick of yours gave you the go-ahead to bed me doesn't mean I've given you the green light, you insufferable, arrogant jerk!"

"Wait a minute. Wait a minute." He grabbed hold of her weapon of choice before she could find a way to inflict injury with it. "What the hell is going on here? I was teasing!"

Jane stopped short and glowered at him. "I am not laughing."

"I can see that." He wasn't laughing anymore, either. Her chest heaved, her hair tumbled about her shoulders in a glorious riot of sunshine, and her eyes were on fire. He knew he should look away before he did something stupid. He just couldn't bring himself to.

Before the rational part of his brain could kick in, he pulled her into his arms, claiming her lips with a ferocity that startled them both. She tasted like honey. She fit perfectly into him, as if some divine being had chiseled her especially for Devon McAlister.

For one magnificent moment, everything in Devon's world felt right. Nothing mattered except drawing her nearer unto him. And then she wrenched herself away and smacked him soundly upside the head with that damned pillow again. He yanked it from her hands and tossed it across the cabin.

The pair squared off: him in his boxers with his feet planted firmly, a defiant scowl on his face; her still kneeling on the bed, her eyes alight with radiant fury. His breath came in great gulps; He felt like he was drowning. He wanted to reach out and grab her again more than anything he'd ever wanted in his life. It was excruciating. It was exhilarating.

Jane was the first to move, her lithe arms reaching out to pull him to her. This time it was her mouth greedily exploring him. They fell back on the bed, a tangled web of arms and legs. His large hands ran along her ribs to span her small waist, then on to the gentle curve of her hips. She alternated between clutching him to her and running her hands along his muscled arms and down his back, her fingertips leaving a trail of electricity in their wake.

The fire threatened to swallow him whole. The animalistic need surging from the pit of him wanted nothing more than to touch and taste her fully. Something in the very back of his mind told him to stop. For reasons he'd never fully understand, he listened to that quiet voice telling him to pull back.

His kiss tapered off to one of quiet reverence. He took her face in his hands. "I shouldn't have done that. I'm sorry."

"I have no idea what came over me." Jane sounded horrified.

"It was delightful. Unexpected, but delightful."

"I might have been giving off some mixed signals just then." Jane tried to scoot away from him, but Devon threw a leg over her and pulled her back to him.

"Slightly, yes, but we'll chalk it up to exhaustion. I promise I just came over here to feed you lunch. I really did undress you so your clothes could dry. I wasn't trying to bed you."

"I'd hate to see what happened if you did try."

Devon couldn't for the life of him think of a safe reply, so he kissed her temple and held silent.

"I can't believe I did that." Jane rubbed her forehead with her fingers. It was the same gesture she made the night they first met. Devon thought it was ridiculously cute.

"I don't know what all you heard between me and Cass." Devon hoped he wouldn't regret broaching the topic but plunged ahead anyway. "But it couldn't have been the whole conversation. If it had been, then you'd know I respect you too much to ever treat you like that."

"What do you see this as being?" Jane shifted so she could prop herself up on one arm. "Are you trying to tell me you are actually interested in starting a lasting, committed relationship with me?"

Devon blinked, unsure how to respond.

"Don't panic, Devon. I'm not looking for a relationship either. It's the last thing on my mind, trust me. But I also don't believe in bed hopping, so I steer clear of the whole game. That's really why everyone calls me a nun behind my back."

"I don't bed hop."

"No disrespect intended," she promised. "Whatever you call it, I don't think it's good for you, and I don't see how it could possibly be fulfilling."

"There is no way for me to respond to that without getting in trouble," Devon protested. "And I'm trying really hard not to be offended."

"You can't possibly be making love to those women. You're having sex, which is nowhere near as fulfilling."

"Do enlighten me." Devon couldn't decide if he was intrigued or angry.

"When's the last time you got so close to someone you felt like your soul touched theirs?"

They both knew the answer; he didn't bother to verbalize it. Instead he turned the question back on her. "When's the last time you did?"

Tears filled her eyes, effectively taking his heart and squeezing it nearly in two. "It's been a few years now, but I trusted my soul to the wrong person. I guess I can't judge, huh? Not sure one is better than the other."

Devon quietly searched her eyes. He'd never been a particularly violent man, but he had a sudden urge to find the one who'd hurt Jane and beat him – severely. He did the only thing that seemed at all right: He hugged her. She tensed for a fraction of a second before snuggling down further into the safety of his arms. He could have stayed in that moment forever, but her stomach rumbled, reminding him that she still hadn't eaten.

"Wait right here," Devon instructed, pleasantly surprised when she complied. He gathered up a new plate for both of them and climbed back in bed with her.

"Thank you." She gratefully accepted the food this time. He held the plate between them and they ate in silence. He couldn't chat; he was too busy processing everything that had transpired between them. He assumed she was doing the same.

"I had appendicitis." Jane broke the silence. "By the time they did the surgery, it had already scarred my fallopian tubes. That's why I can't have kids."

"I'm sorry." They seemed like feeble words, but they were all he had.

"It was really important to Sam to have kids. I mean, that was a pretty big part of his plan for life."

"Are you saying your boyfriend left you because you couldn't have children anymore?" Devon thought he'd surely misunderstood her.

"He was my fiancé." Jane's voice sounded small.

Devon's fist clenched. He'd give anything to have five minutes alone in a room with this Sam. He doubted a rage-filled rant was what Jane needed from him at the moment, though. "Janey, I don't know what to say. What can I do?"

"That's the second time you've called me Janey."

"It just seemed to fit. Do you not like it?"

"My family calls me that sometimes. I don't mind."

"Would you like me to make a few phone calls?" Devon offered, not fully joking. "What does this ass do for a living? I'll have him ruined by nightfall."

"He's a youth pastor making about twenty grand a year. You'd hurt the teenagers he works with more than him."

"Oh." Devon was sorely disappointed. "That seems like a bad career fit. He shouldn't be molding young minds.... Can I at least punch him on my next trip to the States?"

"I'm trying to take a Micah 6:8 approach to the whole thing myself."

"And that is?"

"Look it up."

"Really? You aren't going to just tell me?" Devon chuckled. She had to be joking.

"Nope." She was serious.

"You're meaner than you look."

"Yep."

They fell silent again. When they finished off the first plate of food, Devon got up to snag seconds. As he sifted through the multitude of feelings tumbling through him, he realized there was another new one to add to the list of firsts: fear. He was dangerously close to caring if Jane stuck around or not, and that scared the hell out of him.

CHAPTER TEN

RAIN FELL STEADILY OUTSIDE, tapping out a soothing rhythm on the roof. For a moment, it struck Jane how surreal the moment was. She, prudish Jane Russell, was in her underwear, draped over a similarly clad man she barely knew. As passionate as their brief make-out session had been, all she felt now was comfortable and safe. Okay, so there was a little more than that coursing through her, but those were the feelings that dominated the moment.

Maybe Jane was imagining it, but it seemed they both understood their intentions were too mismatched to ever allow them to be lovers, yet neither seemed ready to walk away from whatever was happening between them at this snapshot in time.

So she enjoyed her time in his arms, knowing it was finite. She wondered how she'd ever been indifferent toward Devon McAlister. It was crazy how quickly he became the center of her thoughts and desires. Still, she'd been immune to him once before. Surely she could figure out how to do it again, later.

A bag of rice on the counter vibrated, making Jane jump. Devon's lip twitched in amusement.

"That's my phone. I can't believe it's working already." He slid out from under her to answer it. It was obvious from his half of the conversation that Aldo had returned to the house and alerted the others as to what had happened. Jane felt a measure of guilt that she'd completely forgotten how worried everyone would be about them. Devon promised the person on the other end they were okay and would be back once the rain passed.

The call was sufficient to ground her in reality. Jane gathered the covers around her self-consciously.

"So the moment's gone, then?" Devon surmised, setting the phone on the counter.

"It's probably best. Right?" A tiny piece of Jane wished he'd say no, that he'd take her in his arms and tell her he was a changed man. But the realist in Jane knew that no woman on the planet had ever successfully changed a man, not really. It was something he either did on his own or not at all.

"You are unlike any woman I've ever met." He came to sit on the edge of the bed beside her and took her hands in his. "Thank you for today. I know this is going to sound crazy since we were almost killed and all, but I enjoyed it... this time with you."

"You're welcome." Jane wanted him so badly it ached. She'd never in her life felt anything remotely close to the yearning that permeated her at that moment.

He cupped the back of her head with his hand and gave her one last lingering kiss. Jane barely suppressed her whimper in response.

After that kiss, Jane knew she wasn't imagining his withdrawal from her. For the rest of the day, he was both friendly and chivalrous, but there was an unmistakable formality and distance, too. Jane was thankful for it; she wasn't sure she'd have been able to maintain the space between them all on her own.

The walk back to the main house reminded Jane she needed to get back into shape. Her lungs protested the exertion more than they should have. The air was sticky after the rain. Jane spent her walk thinking about getting cleaned up more than anything else. She followed Devon silently, dreaming of a shower and clean pajamas.

The reception when they arrived at the house was mixed. The majority of the household greeted them with smiles or even hugs, but Cass's expression was stern at best. She looked at Jane like she was little better than trash. Jane knew what the woman thought had happened while they were away. Did she and Devon look guilty, or did Cass just assume the worst? Indignation and shame warred within Jane under the other woman's hate-filled glare.

After checking on the cubs, Jane excused herself for that shower she'd been wanting. Then she put on some loose yoga pants and a camisole, fully intending to hide in her room for the rest of the night. Lucia brought her dinner, and Jane surprised her with a warm hug in return.

It had been a long day. So much had happened; so much had changed. She was scared for her life, her heart, and her livelihood. She wished she could talk to her cousin Charlie. He had such a level head; he'd know what to do, or he'd at least listen to her without judging. Charlie's wife, Neena, would give her a hug and tell her it was all going to be okay. Maybe that's what she really needed at the moment, someone to hug her and tell her everything would be alright again someday.

Jane had just finished scrawling all of those thoughts and fears into her journal when there was a tap at the door. She was surprised to see Devon.

"Do you want to come in?" Jane leaned against the door, making room for him to step past.

His eyes raked over her. He cleared his throat. "I'd better not."

She nodded and kept her hands planted on the door behind her, lest they reach out on their own accord.

"I'm sorry," he blurted after an awkward pause. "I saw the look Cass was giving you earlier. I've spoken to her about it. I told her it wasn't her business but that nothing happened between us."

Jane's heart thumped painfully as the words *nothing happened between us* echoed in her mind. Outwardly, she gave him a small smile. "Thank you."

"Until we know what happened today, who was at the preserve, I think it's probably best if we stay close to the house. Is there anything over there you absolutely need?"

Jane shook her head. "Not that I can think of. Do you have any idea what's going on?"

"I have a few theories but none worth sharing yet. I'll do some asking around. I don't plan to just hand over your preserve without a fight, but it might take me a little time to put together a game plan."

Jane bit her lower lip and studied his face. He was so handsome and sincere. Her fingers itched to touch him. "Why are you doing this? You are going so far beyond neighborly."

Devon shrugged self-consciously. "It's the right thing to do."

"You really mean that, don't you? I misjudged you, Devon. I'm sorry about that."

"I'm sure it's not the first time. Someone misjudged me, I mean. Not that you've misjudged someone. Why do I sound like such an idiot around you?"

Jane stifled a giggle. "Goodnight, Devon."

"Goodnight, Jane."

That night, her dreams weren't of unknown assailants or angry assistants. They were wholly and completely Devon McAlister's.

The next morning, she allowed herself five minutes to stretch out her toes and happily relive those dreams. Then she rose, dressed, and set her mind to reclaiming that distance between them—as best was possible while living under the same roof, that is.

As it turned out, distance wasn't too difficult to maintain with Devon buried in his office. If he didn't have his nose stuck in a report, he was out at the packaging plant or in one of his greenhouses. The man was never still.

Just when Jane thought she'd found her equilibrium, Devon joined them for breakfast, throwing everything askew again. Devon, Jane, Maria, Aldo, and Cass all struggled to make small talk, although each for different reasons. When the gate intercom buzzed, Devon looked almost relieved for the interruption.

"Are you expecting someone?" He glanced at Cass, who shook her head. He excused himself to go see who it was while the others waited anxiously. Jane reminded herself that the gunmen from the day before wouldn't buzz the gate for entrance, but that thought didn't reassure her much.

The clock on the wall ticked loudly. Jane couldn't stand listening to it anymore so she tried once more to start a conversation. "So Cass, how long have you worked for Devon?"

"A long time." She didn't bother to look up.

"Where are you from originally?"

"Virginia." Cass stabbed a banana piece.

"I've never been to Virginia. I've heard it's lovely, though."

"You can stop trying to befriend me." Cass dropped her fork and leveled her gaze on Jane. "You aren't going to get to him through me."

"I wasn't trying to get to anyone through you." Jane dropped her own fork and met Cass's stare. "I was merely being nice. I'm not surprised to find it's such a foreign concept for you that you don't even recognize it."

"Devon has a lot of people depending on him," Cass hissed. "The last thing he needs is to be distracted by your little drama."

"I get it." Jane took a deep breath and reminded herself to have a shred of compassion for the woman. "I know you have feelings for Devon, but that's a conversation you need to have with him. Stop taking it out on me, though. I've done absolutely nothing to you."

Maria and Aldo exchanged uncomfortable glances.

"Or you could go play damsel in distress for someone else and leave him out of it," Cass countered.

Jane rose slowly, planting her hands on the table and leaning closer to Cass before she spoke, her tone deadly calm. "I'll make you a deal, lady. I'll stop trying to be nice to you, and you leave me alone. No more condescending looks or nasty little comments. I'm a human being, not a hunk of trash. If you can't grasp that, I pity you, but leave me out of your neurosis."

Jane continued to stare at Cass for a full minute, everything in her body language shouting she'd be happy to brawl about it if need be. Cass averted her gaze, her glare shifting to a look of horror when she did. Jane turned to see what Cass was looking at, only to find a very surprised Devon along with an amused stranger who seemed vaguely familiar.

"How long have you been there?" Jane felt a wave of guilt; she hadn't intended to humiliate Cass.

"We just walked in." Devon was lying. Jane could see it all over his face.

"We were in earshot long enough to know Cass hails from Virginia, though," the stranger supplied, earning a punch in the shoulder from Devon.

"I'm so sorry." Jane turned to Cass, who burst from the table and rushed from the room. Jane turned helplessly to Devon. "I'm sorry. I didn't mean to embarrass her. I just hit my wall. I was just trying to be nice when I started the conversation. I really was."

"Hey, hey." Devon crossed the distance between them to place his hands on Jane's shoulders. "It's okay. I know you don't have a mean bone in your body. I can imagine how it started. I'll smooth it over with Cassandra later."

Tears welled in Jane's eyes. She felt horrible about the whole mess, and to have it happen in front of a total stranger was just too much.

"Come here." He pulled her into a hug. "Don't worry about it. Why don't you go check on the cubs and meet me back here in a few minutes? I have some updates for you."

Jane knew full well that Lucia had already fed the cubs breakfast, and Devon knew it, too. He was giving her an excuse to go pull herself together. She was grateful for it.

She was nearly to the stall before she realized Maria had excused herself, too. The two women stood in silence for a couple of minutes, simply watching the babies sleep. Jane sniffed and tried not to think about how mortified she was over her public display.

"Are you okay?" Maria finally asked.

Jane nodded. "The past few days have just been pretty stressful. I think it's starting to get to me."

"And Mr. McAlister, is he being good to you?"

"He's been wonderful to me," Jane assured her friend. "We're just very different people looking for very different things in life. Tell poor Aldo not to hang up his matchmaking hat just yet."

Maria placed an arm over Jane's shoulders and gave her a squeeze. "It's going to be okay, *mi hija.*"

"Thank you. I really needed to hear that," Jane confessed. "We'd better get back. I've made enough of a spectacle of myself this morning."

"You weren't the spectacle and everyone knows it," Maria insisted.

The two women linked arms and ambled back to the dining room. Jane knew she should be more eager for an update, and she was curious what the stranger knew about their situation, but she was also loath to face the men again. She did so with her head held high, though.

"How are your charges?" Devon asked her brightly as she reclaimed her seat.

"Sleeping." Jane returned his smile. They exchanged a look that made everything seem alright again. "They looked pretty fat and happy to me. I think Lucia has been taking good care of them."

"I'm Cody," the stranger drawled, leaning toward Jane. He was seated to Devon's left, enjoying breakfast as if he'd been part of the group all along. "I don't know if Devon here had any plans to introduce me to you lovely ladies."

"Jane, Maria, this is Senator Kingsley. He's a horrible flirt, so keep an eye on him."

"I am not a horrible flirt; I'm actually quite good at it."

"But not at jokes," Jane interjected, amused. Now she knew why the man had seemed familiar. The senator from Texas was in the news often. He was handsome and charismatic, and the media loved him. Most said he'd be presidential candidate material if he ever settled down and got married. That knowledge should have bridled Jane's tongue, but she was rather enjoying the banter. It was a refreshing break from the emotional wringer of the past several days.

"Ouch. You wounded me deeply just then." Cody clutched his heart and gave her a beseeching look. "Are you really already so far gone over this rake that I don't stand a chance?"

"Who says rake anymore?" Jane tossed back. "And I'm not gone over anybody, but you don't stand a chance regardless."

Her eyes faltered when they locked with Devon's. What did she see there? Surely he wasn't offended – they'd both been abundantly clear that it wasn't meant to be.

"Uh huh." Cody's grin was mischievous. "Well, it is a pleasure to meet you ladies. When I came to visit dear old Devon, I had no idea I was in for such a treat."

"If you're finished trying to hit on my neighbor, maybe you could fill them in on what you told me." Devon's voice lacked humor.

"I have some... associates... who work with me on some of the lesser-known initiatives of the current administration. Without going into undue detail, one of them intercepted some communications that led me to believe my old friend here has stumbled into a hornet's nest." Cody's southern drawl was even more accentuated. He seemed to be proceeding carefully, searching for the right words.

"By helping us," Jane surmised.

"It sounds like both properties were in the middle of the hornet's nest to begin with," Devon corrected. "It was just dumb luck they chose yours and not mine."

"Or the fact that you're rich and important," Jane sighed. "They didn't expect anybody to notice or care if the Guerreros and I disappeared.

"Was that an accusation?" Devon got defensive.

Cody watched them like they were participating in a tennis match. Aldo and Maria exchanged another glance.

"Not at all." Jane quickly shook her head. "Just a statement of fact. If anything, it speaks to your character. You could have ignored our plight."

"We've been over this...." Devon began, only to be interrupted by Jane.

"Cody, do you have any idea who it is that's decided to take over the preserve's land?"

"Well, now, that's the fun part." Cody fidgeted with his fork before glancing around the table. "There are three properties that make up the bulk of this area: Devon's plantation, the jaguar preserve, and an estate that belongs to a man named Javier Barrera."

"I'll kill him." Devon's voice was menacing and low.

"I've heard the locals talking about him." Jane glanced over at Maria and Aldo. She could tell by their expressions they'd already suspected as much. "He's a drug lord, isn't he?"

"You had to know it was him," Cody spoke to Devon. "You knew who your neighbor was when you bought the place."

"I suspected him until one of the jaguars was killed."

"What does Deifilia have to do with it?" Jane interjected.

"Barrera has a thing for big cats. He collects them. If Deifilia had been stolen, that I could see him doing. But I didn't expect him to kill her."

"That was one of his men. My sources tell me Javier had someone executed just after the attack. Apparently there is another man missing."

"Why now?" Devon asked.

"It's complicated. The short version is that drug enforcement clamped down on its usual trade routes. My guess is that Barrera needed to find another way to move his product rather than risk missing his quota."

"Drug lords have quotas?" Jane couldn't help jumping in.

"They do if they've climbed in bed with Hezbollah," Cody replied quietly. All traces of humor were gone as he turned to Devon. "If you strap Barrera on by yourself, you'll bring down the wrath of hell on this plantation. They'll blow it off the map, and every one of your workers with it. You and I both know it."

CHAPTER ELEVEN

DEVON FELT LIKE HE'D BEEN PUNCHED in the gut. He'd heard rumors that Hezbollah was funding its terrorist endeavors across the globe through operations in the Western hemisphere, but he hadn't realized just how close to home it had gotten. "I thought they were in Venezuela. Brazil, maybe. But Ecuador?"

"They're like cockroaches. For every one you see, there's a thousand more hidden in the walls. We're only now beginning to get our arms around just how big a problem this is," Cody answered.

"I'm sorry; I don't mean to be the slow one here." Jane held up her hand. "But I thought Hezbollah was the terrorist group out of Iran."

"That's the one," Cody confirmed.

"So terrorists took over the preserve?" Aldo summarized.

"Not exactly. We haven't confirmed that there are any terrorist cells functioning in Ecuador to date; it's purely a financial transaction so far. I'm not sure if anyone from Iran is even on the ground in Ecuador at this point, but the cyber trail definitely links Barrera to the group, which means if you pick a fight with him, they will protect their interests. This is their foot in the door to this country. They won't easily give it up." Cody looked around the table.

Devon knew his friend well enough to know that if he'd been concerned enough to get on a plane and fly five hours to come warn him, there was more going on here than he probably wanted to know. "Oh crap." He paled. "Alex is on her way here with her family."

"When are you expecting her?" The concern barely flickered across Cody's face before he recovered his composure.

"They're spending some time with friends stateside, in Missouri, right now. They fly down day after tomorrow. Is it safe to call her?"

"I wouldn't, not on unsecured phone lines" Cody shook his head. "I think the best thing you can do is go about business as normal. As far as anyone is concerned, I'm here to talk rare earth minerals with you and your sister. I'll rearrange my schedule to be here while she is. I might even drop in on Javier to be social. As far as he's concerned, I have no clue what's going on. I don't think he'll make a move on you while I'm here."

"So we're going to spend the next week pretending there is nothing wrong?" Jane clarified.

"Pretty much." Cody grinned at her, his easygoing demeanor returning.

"Is there anything else we can do?" Aldo spoke up. "Is there anything we can do to repay you, Mr. McAlister?"

"We don't feel right about being such a burden," Maria added.

"You're not a burden at all. The furthest thing from it, actually," Devon promised her with a kind smile. He genuinely liked the couple. "If you truly want something to do to make the time pass, I'm positive Pablo and Lucia have plenty of projects they'd appreciate help on. But I'd rather you consider yourselves guests."

"You're not putting me to work, McAlister." Cody threw his hands up. "Don't even think about it."

"You're a politician. He knows better," Jane teased.

"Vixen," Cody laughingly accused. "You really ought to forget about Devon. He couldn't handle a woman as feisty as you."

"I'm not a racehorse."

"Of course not. You don't have the legs for it." Cody raised his eyebrows at her as if anticipating her response.

"Cretin."

"Flatterer."

Jane opened her mouth to reply but sighed and shook her head instead. Devon watched the exchange, yet another unfamiliar feeling bubbling under the surface of his cool façade: jealousy. He didn't care how long he and Cody Kingsley had been friends or how badly he needed the man's help. Devon was going to pummel him if he had to watch this exchange any longer.

He shoved himself back from the table. "I'd better go talk to Cass, and then I have some work to see to before Alex and her family arrive this week. I trust you'll all make yourselves at home."

After a round of polite goodbyes, Devon left the room, but not before he overheard Jane eagerly accept an invitation from Cody to tour the rose operations. He paused for half a beat before mentally ordering himself to just keep walking.

He fumed the entire walk to Cass's little cottage. He understood that he and Jane were better off apart, but he didn't understand how Kingsley was a better choice for her. Devon wondered what Cody had that he didn't. Was it the accent? Surely a woman as intelligent as Jane wouldn't be swayed by a southern twang.

Devon stopped for a minute, leaning against the railing on Cass's front porch to clear his head before knocking on her door. This was going to be a difficult enough conversation without him already being out of sorts.

When Cass opened the door, her red eyes and splotchy face gave away that she'd been crying. Devon felt like a total ass. How had he missed her feelings for him?

"Do you have a minute?" He nodded toward the bench in her garden.

"You can come in if you want," she offered.

"It's a pretty day out." He headed toward the garden. He might have been obtuse enough to miss her intentions to begin with, but now that he knew them, he wasn't taking any chances at sending mixed signals.

They sat down at opposite ends of the wrought iron bench. After thinking for a second about how best to start, Devon turned toward Cass, his voice gentle. "What Jane said, about your feelings for me, was that true?"

Cass didn't answer, not verbally anyway. Her back was ramrod straight, her hands folded primly in her lap, and her head was bent in defeat.

Devon didn't like it one little bit. The Cass he knew, the woman who was his friend and most trusted employee, was never defeated. "I am so sorry. I had no idea."

"You mean you never noticed it, how amazing we are together?"

"We do work well together; we're a great team, but that doesn't mean there's something there romantically. Cass, I'm your boss."

"Then I quit."

"I wish you wouldn't, because you're a fantastic employee. Quitting isn't going to change how I feel, though."

"It's her," Cass accused, narrowing her eyes.

"I can't say I even begin to understand what's going on between me and Jane, but if this had come up before I met her, my answer would have been the same." It pained Devon to hurt Cassandra. On more than one occasion, he'd have been lost without her. But lying or even tiptoeing around the truth would only prolong her misery.

"I can't do it. I won't do it." Cass folded her arms across her chest and shook her head. "You don't have a clue what I've done for you – and now you want me to sit by and watch you trip all over yourself for her?"

Devon took exception to that. He didn't think he'd been exactly tripping over himself. Had he? "Why don't you take some time off?" he suggested. "Give yourself a week or two on a beach somewhere before you make any major life decisions. It'll be my treat."

"You're sending me away?"

"Not at all."

"You are. You're sending me away so you don't feel so guilty about being with her." Her voice was rife with accusation.

"What do you want from me?" Devon was dangerously close to exploding.

"You. I want you."

"That's not going to happen, Cass. Even if Jane goes home tomorrow, that's not going to happen."

"Where does that leave us?"

"I really think we need some time to figure that out. Please, take the keys to the house in San Clemente. Go pamper yourself for a couple of weeks. Think about what you want to do next. Then we'll see what we can figure out from there."

It took a few more minutes of convincing, but Cass finally agreed to go. Devon had no clue how the place would function with her gone, and he didn't even want to contemplate what this whole fiasco meant long term, but he'd worry about that later. First, he had to get his lovelorn assistant out the door, keep the philandering senator from seducing his virtuous neighbor, keep them all from being killed by terrorists, and prepare his house for a visit from royalty.

It was shaping up to be one hell of a day. He intended to work from his home office rather than have to watch Cody and Jane and all the shameless flirting going on, but somehow his feet didn't listen to him, and he found himself on the path leading over to the farm's packaging plant.

According to his foreman, his guests had already been there and had moved on to the greenhouses. To his horror, Devon contemplated following them. He'd been looking forward to being the one to show Jane his roses, especially some of the rarer varieties they had in development. His roses brought him great joy. Regardless of the status of their relationship or lack thereof, he'd wanted to share that joy with her.

Unaware of the battle going on inside his boss's head, the foreman took advantage of having Devon around and began rattling off the list of things he'd been saving for their next encounter. It was over an hour later before Devon was able to extract himself, and even then it was only with the promise to follow up again within the week.

Naturally, Jane was long gone from the greenhouses by the time Devon made his way there. Once again, he found himself cornered by a supervisor who'd been waiting for answers on a bevy of topics. It was the same in every greenhouse, and in the clerical office. Just as he wrapped up the conversation with his accountant, he was stopped by one of his newer employees.

"*Señor* McAlister." The young woman flagged him down from the door of the daycare.

He dutifully crossed the yard to see what she needed, wracking his brain as he did, trying to remember her name.

"Thank you so much for the job, *Señor* McAlister. If you need anything at all, just tell me." She gratefully shook his hand. The toddler clinging to her leg worked up the nerve to peek past her skirt to study Devon. He waved at the boy, who buried his face back in his mother's skirt.

"It's my pleasure." He wished he could remember her name. "We're happy to have you as part of the team."

"My grocery account is all set up now, and Sebastian is all settled in at school."

"I'm glad to hear it. If you ever need anything, my door is always open. Well, if you can find me. I'm afraid I'm not here as often as I'd like to be," he admitted. It took five more minutes of polite conversation before he could take his leave.

Under normal circumstances, he enjoyed visiting with his employees, and he certainly liked knowing they were well and taken care of, but it was nearing dinnertime and he was exhausted. He was also feeling guilty for not paying enough attention to the rose plantation. Things had been busy for McAlister Industries for the last couple of years, even more so once they ventured into the mineral industry. His sister, Alex, did her best to keep up with that aspect of the business, but with a growing family to raise and the extra responsibilities her unique family brought, she hadn't been as much help as she'd like to be. His half-sister, Karise, wasn't a McAlister, and though she'd been welcomed into the McAlister fold, she wanted nothing to do with that side of her family.

Devon supposed it was little wonder he'd never gotten around to settling down with one woman, no matter how often Alex got after him to do so. Now that she was happily married, she thought everyone should be. Some days it felt like the weight of the world was on his shoulders, with so many families depending on him to make good decisions so they could continue to put food on their tables. It had been Cass's steady presence that made it possible. He didn't know how he was going to manage with that relationship irrevocably fractured.

He was surly as he trudged back up the path to the main house. He needed a stiff drink and a hot bath. Since both were probably several hours away still, he decided to swing by the stables to visit the cubs.

Devon could hear their laughter before he even passed the first stall. He debated turning back; he wasn't sure he was up to seeing them together. Maybe it was a streak of masochism that propelled him on.

Jane was enchanting as always, sitting against the wall on the stall floor with Aria in her lap. Her hair broke free from the loose ponytail to tumble about her shoulders. Laughter danced in her eyes as the cub toyed with Jane's hand. Freya rolled around nearby, tussling with a dog toy. Cody sat perched on the window ledge, watching Jane with amusement.

The pair was so caught up in their easy conversation that they didn't notice Devon at first. He propped his arms on the wooden half-door and leaned into the stall. "Did you enjoy your tour?" His voice was light—at least, he hoped it was.

"Very much." Jane's enthusiasm made him wish even more he'd been the one to show her.

"Did you see the yellow ones with red and orange tinges? Those are my favorite." They reminded Devon of Jane. He'd decided that today on his own tour of the greenhouses.

"I must have missed them."

"Maybe next time." Devon studied her face, looking for some clue as to how she felt about Cody. Had her day been good because it had been spent with him?

"I loved the reds, though. Such pretty, vibrant shades. It was fascinating to see how they're grown. Thank you for letting us explore."

Devon was delighted at her compliment. He didn't have the first clue what to say now without making a total fool of himself in front of Cody, though, so he merely nodded in response.

"Oh, Devon, I almost forgot," Cody interjected, his obvious amusement at the situation irritating Devon. "Lucia said to tell you that dinner is at seven tonight on the patio."

"Thanks," Devon acknowledged, glad he'd have time for that bath and drink after all. "I guess I'll let you two get back to your conversation, then."

He walked away, struggling with yet another new feeling: rejection. He didn't like this one at all. It was even worse than the jealousy or fear. If this was what it felt like to fall in love, Devon decided he was better off with his meaningless affairs. At least they left him feeling satiated and confident, which was infinitely more appealing than his current state of restless need and utter ineptitude.

CHAPTER TWELVE

AS JANE WATCHED DEVON WALK AWAY, she wondered what was bothering him. He was obviously preoccupied and unhappy. She worried his conversation with Cass hadn't gone well and was causing even more stress than he was already under. She wished she could wave some magic wand and make it all go away for him. Maybe it would help him to talk about all the burdens he was shouldering— if only she could control herself around him long enough to have a conversation.

"You two are something else," Cody declared.

"What's that supposed to mean?" Jane stopped staring at the empty space where Devon had been and turned to Cody.

"It never ceases to amaze me how intelligent people can be so stupid when it comes to love."

"I barely know Devon," Jane protested. "Granted, I find him attractive, kind, and enjoyable to be around, but he and I couldn't be more different. We've both agreed it's best to stay friends and no more."

"Right." The way Cody drew out the word said he didn't believe it for one second. "Like I said...."

"And I suppose you're the love wizard," she retorted. "I've heard too much about your escapades to take any advice from you seriously."

"You know what they say about assumptions," he cautioned.

"Alright then, prove me wrong."

"I was in love once," he countered, his eyes growing distant. "I suppose I still am, but she hates me."

"I doubt she truly hates you. You're quite charming; I imagine it would be hard to stay angry with you for long."

"No, she really hates me. She tells me on a regular basis."

"So you still have contact with her?" Jane was curious about the woman who had such a firm hold on Cody's heart. How had the media never caught wind of that one?

"We work together. She avoids me when possible. I randomly try to win her forgiveness. Then she threatens to kill me. Given her line of work, I'm not entirely sure it's an idle threat."

"She sounds lovely."

"She is." Cody meant his simple statement; Jane could tell by the look in his eyes that he loved this woman very much.

"Do you want to tell me about her?"

"I just might take you up on that sometime." Cody hopped down from his perch and dusted himself off. "But now, I'm going to see if I can squeeze a horseback ride in before dinner. Care to join me?"

"I don't ride." Jane set Aria in the straw and accepted Cody's hand up. "But thank you anyway. Have fun."

Jane had enjoyed her time with Cody, both because he was easy to like and because she'd loved learning so much about Devon's home and business. Still, she was glad for some time alone to process it all. Jane had heard awful things about the rose industry before coming to Ecuador. She'd never believed Devon to be capable of underpaying employees or exposing them to harmful chemicals, but today she realized that, even then, she hadn't given him enough credit.

Not only was his plantation environmentally friendly and sustainably run, but he went above and beyond when it came to taking care of his employees. He paid well above the normal local wage, provided free onsite daycare and advancement programs, and even paid a portion of their wages in a grocery account so alcoholic husbands couldn't drink the women's earnings away. Once a month, he brought in a doctor to see his employees and their children for free.

And his eyes lit up like a child at Christmas at the mention of his favorite rose color. The more she learned about Devon, the more fascinated she became. Ever since she first took the time to get to know him, Jane had realized how wrong she'd been to judge him. Now she was beginning to grasp just how wrong. It seemed Devon's kindness and generosity didn't come from some sense of morality or obligation; he truly cared about these people and wanted to give them a better life.

Jane wasn't the kind of woman to try to catch a man, and she was still fully aware of the folly in trying to forge any kind of relationship with Devon, but that didn't stop her from wanting to look pretty for him at dinner that night. For the next hour, she took great care in bathing, shaving, fixing her hair, picking the perfect sundress, and even putting on a splash of the makeup she found in Alex's bathroom.

The reflection in the mirror told her she was as ready as she'd ever be. The white dress clung to her soft curves, hinting at what lie beneath the gauzy fabric. She'd twisted some of her hair into a barrette but allowed most of it to tumble about as it pleased. A hint of mascara accentuated the lashes that framed her large green eyes. Pink lip stain gave her full lips a just-kissed look. She even braved a pair of strappy heels that accented the clean lines of her slender calves.

When she made her entrance on the patio that night, she was pleased to get a double-take from Devon. But then, after devouring her with his eyes, he turned away, scowling. She wanted to run away crying. She turned around to do just that when she was intercepted by Cody, who took her by the elbow and gave her an appreciative once-over.

He let out a low whistle and grinned. "Good God, Jane, you look amazing."

"Thank you." Jane flushed with pleasure. It might be the wrong man, but at least someone thought her effort had been worthwhile.

"You look lovely," Maria whispered as they took their seats.

"Thanks." Jane was beginning to feel self-conscious. Maybe it had been too much of a change. When Aldo commented on her appearance, too, Devon's scowl deepened even further and Jane felt even more like an idiot.

The patio was decked out in preparation for Alex's arrival. Pablo had hung lights to complement the riots of flowers gracing the pillars and rafters. Latin-flavored music played in the background. After dinner was cleared away, the small party lingered outside over wine to enjoy the ambience and temperate night air.

"I don't suppose I could sweet-talk you into dancing with me?" Cody turned pleading eyes on Jane.

"Why not?" she decided impetuously. Between the dress, the night air, and the wine, it seemed like the thing to do. She didn't know the steps to the dance he chose or even what it was called, but he was a good teacher, and he was forgiving when she stepped on his toes. By the end of the song, they were both laughing so hard their sides hurt, but they managed to earn a round of applause from Aldo and Maria, who decided to join them on their impromptu dance floor for the next song.

The song had barely begun when Devon stormed from the table and strode off the patio to the lower gardens. Jane frowned, watching him leave.

"You know," Cody murmured against her ear, "it won't offend me if you go see what's wrong."

"You're pretty fantastic, you know that?" Jane gave him a quick kiss on the cheek before going after Devon. She forced herself to walk at a sedate pace. Partly so she wouldn't look too pathetic racing after him; partly so she wouldn't fall flat on her face. She still wasn't used to the heels.

"Hey, wait up," Jane called when she gave up on catching him.

Devon halted and turned to her. In two good strides, he was standing in front of her, close enough that she could feel the tension radiating off him. "I thought you didn't like to dance."

"I don't."

"You seemed to be enjoying yourself."

"That's different. I don't know. I was just being silly; I felt like trying something new."

"Like the dress? Did Cody inspire you to try that, too?"

"This inquisition is not endearing you to me," Jane warned.

"Not him, Jane. I get it if you don't want me; I'm not going to beg, but not him. He'll break your heart."

"You hypocrite. Are you seriously warning me that Cody is too much of a player for me?"

"I don't want to see you hurt."

"Do you prefer to do it yourself? Is that it?" Jane was furious.

"Me? I'm the one inflicting pain?"

"You think I am?"

Devon didn't answer. His jaw was clenched and his eyes held hers captive. She struggled to catch her breath under the weight of those eyes. Was Devon McAlister seriously jealous? Over her?

Without a word, he placed a hand on each of her cheeks, tilting her face up to him, then leaned down and kissed her. His touch was surprisingly tender. It stirred such longing in her soul it made her want to cry.

She was vaguely aware that they were still in full view of the patio, but she didn't care. She wrapped her arms around Devon and pressed her body into him, deepening the kiss when he would have pulled away. She wasn't ready to be bereft of his touch.

No, she wanted more. She wanted all of him. His kiss took her to dizzying heights and melted away every last shred of reserve. When he ended it, she rested her head against his chest until the world stopped spinning. Neither spoke at first. He rested his chin on the top of her head.

"I don't want your heart to be broken again." His voice sounded sad.

She didn't say anything in return. All she could think was that it was already too late to keep that from happening.

"I'm sorry, I shouldn't have done that," he spoke again.

"Don't. Please. I understand that we're not right for each other, but please don't apologize for that kiss. And don't be jealous of Cody. He's a friend, nothing more." She pulled herself out of his arms and walked away with as much composure as possible before she did something horrifying, like offer a one-night stand.

In her head, Jane knew that no man was worth letting go of who she was. But her heart was willing to bargain just about anything to satiate the need for more of him. Distance was the only way Jane knew to keep herself safe until she could reconcile the two.

The entire next day, Jane did everything she could to steer clear of Devon, though she did take a walk down to the greenhouses to find the yellow rose he'd mentioned. She went to the greenhouse she remembered as housing the plantation's new variegated varieties.

"I'm looking for the yellow ones with orange and red," she told the shift supervisor.

"The Janes," he grinned knowingly.

"Excuse me?"

"*Señor* McAlister finally named them yesterday."

"He named a variety of rose after me?" she asked nobody in particular.

"It looks that way," the gentleman replied, leading her to the back of the greenhouse. "We don't have many of them; it's been a hard variety to perfect. He wanted just the right amount of color, just the right shades."

"They're breathtaking." Jane was in awe of their exquisite beauty. Yellow the color of sunshine served as the backdrop; swirls of sultry red and deep orange accented each petal. Their beauty was both happy and complex. The effect was striking.

"I'm sure he'll be pleased to hear you like them."

"Thank you for showing me where they were." Jane knew she should let him get back to work, but she seemed completely unable to tear her eyes away from the roses, her roses. She reached a finger out to gently stroke one of the petals; it felt like silk.

"Careful, those are my most prized flower." Devon's voice surprised her at its nearness. She jumped, nearly bumping into a tray of flowers before he reached out to steady her.

"Sorry. You startled me."

"I can take it from here," Devon informed the employee, who nodded and disappeared with a sly smile.

"They're beautiful." Jane turned back to the roses when the look Devon gave her threatened to leave her a puddle at his feet.

"They are." His breath tickled her ear. His low voice held promise.

A million butterflies exploded into flight in her stomach. "Thank you."

"For what?" he teased. "You didn't think I named them after you, did you?"

Jane whirled to look at him, believing him for half a second. When she saw the mischief in his eyes, she shoved playfully at his chest. "That wasn't nice."

"Probably not," he admitted, laughing before reaching around her to pluck one of the roses from its plant.

For that brief moment, his arms were on either side of her, his body pressed against hers as he clipped the rose's stem. He presented her the rose, followed by a gentle kiss that barely brushed her lips. "Be careful of the thorns."

And then he left her standing there, holding the flower and wondering how long it would be before she could safely walk again. She held the rose to her chest and inhaled deeply, relishing its rich fragrance. Jane remembered where she was and glanced around guiltily, sending every worker in the place skittering back to work.

With a sheepish laugh, she shook her head to clear it before making her way out of the greenhouse. Jane knew she was acting like a starry-eyed teenager, but she couldn't help it. As she strolled back to the house, terrorists and drug lords were the furthest things from her mind. All she could seem to think about with any clarity was the feel of Devon's body pressed against hers. Except maybe the way shivers ran to the very tips of her toes every time he was close enough to kiss her – that she seemed to be able to focus on pretty well.

After the stress of the week, it felt good to amble along, allowing her mind to roam freely. She was so wrapped up in her decadent daydreams that it took her completely by surprise when she let herself into the house only to find they had company.

"Ah, Jane, you're back." The tension in Devon's voice was palpable despite his cool exterior. "We have a surprise visitor. Have you met our other neighbor, Javier?"

"It took over a year for me to get to know you – do you think I was any better about introducing myself to the other neighbors?" Jane tried to keep her voice light as she stepped toward Barrera with a smile plastered on her face. "It's so good to finally meet you."

They kissed cheeks; the hairs on the back of her neck standing on end when her skin brushed against his. "It's a pleasure. Had I known how lovely you are, I would have introduced myself sooner."

"You're too kind." Jane lowered her eyes demurely as she instinctively moved closer to Devon, who'd already begun to move in her direction. He placed his hand on the small of her back, his solid warmth calming and strengthening her. Jane could feel the tension easing from her shoulders.

Javier took in the exchange, his face clearly showing his interest.

"I was beginning to think you'd gotten yourself lost, Jane my girl," Cody teased her cheerfully.

"Not every woman is as daft as the ones you choose to spend your time with," Jane informed him.

"She has you there," Javier chuckled.

Jane smiled at him outwardly. On the inside, her brain was screaming, "Am I the only one who cares that we're making small talk with the drug lord who destroyed my home?" Just as quickly, she remembered Cody's advice to play dead. If Javier thought they weren't a threat, he just might let them live. She'd never had much of a poker face. If she was going to give a performance that was the slightest bit convincing, she needed a moment to calm her nerves. A drink might help, too.

"If you gentlemen will excuse me, I need to go put my rose in a vase." She held up her prize in explanation. "I'll be right back."

"Of course. Let me show you where they are." Devon had already fallen in step beside her. As they left the room, she could hear Cody teasing them about seeking any excuse to be alone together.

Devon did find her a vase for her flower; he even filled it with water and trimmed the stem to the right length. While he was taking care of her rose, she leaned against the counter, chewing on her thumbnail. "What are we going to do?"

"Just keep doing exactly what you are." There was urgency in Devon's whisper. "He's probably wondering what your next step is. Give him something he can believe to assure him you aren't going to try to take the preserve back. He probably would have already killed us both if Cody weren't here. I have no idea how long that will slow his hand, though."

Cody's and Javier's voices grew louder as the two men neared the kitchen. Devon swept Jane into his arms and planted his lips on hers. Fire instantly streaked through every single one of Jane's nerve endings. She quite happily played her part, kissing him back with fervor.

"What did I tell you? Any excuse to be alone. I have never felt so much like a third wheel in my life," Cody proclaimed as they entered the room.

Jane startled, embarrassed to be caught in Devon's embrace even though that had been the point of the kiss.

"Sorry about that," Devon feigned remorse. "Could I persuade you to stay for dinner, Javier? I promise to be a better host."

"Regrettably, I already have a dinner engagement, but Cody mentioned you have an excellent Scotch on hand. I could be convinced to stay for a drink."

"Absolutely. Right this way." Devon locked his fingers through Jane's, pulling her close to his side as they led the way to his bar.

"Maybe you gentlemen could help me with something," Jane suggested, striking up a conversation once they'd all settled in with their drinks.

"Anything for you, my dear." Cody's drawl was as easy as his smile.

"I'm trying to convince Devon to come with me to San Diego when I take the cubs. He could use a vacation."

Devon did a quick double take before realization settled over his features. Jane wished she'd had time to let him in on it, but this was the best lie she could think of on such short notice.

"The cubs?" Javier raised his eyebrows. "I thought my housekeeper was making it up when she said the cubs were found. I'm so glad to hear that wasn't the case."

"They were really the hope of the preserve, you know," Jane explained. "Now that the buildings are gone and their mother is dead, there just doesn't seem to be much point in starting from scratch when the locals so obviously don't want us here. I've made arrangements for the cubs to be taken into a breeding program in San Diego. They'll be safe there. That's all that really matters."

"So, it was locals who did this to you?" Javier probed further.

"I can't fathom who else it would be." Jane's expression was positively angelic. "They threatened us all the time. I just never thought they'd go through with it."

"That's horrible." Javier shook his head sadly.

"It's vile," Jane agreed. "What kind of man would do something like that? It makes you wonder how they sleep at night."

"Truly." Devon's gaze met Jane's, asserting she'd probably hit a good stopping point.

"So, about San Diego?" Jane batted her eyelashes at him, bringing the conversation back to safer territory.

Devon threw his hands up in mock defeat. "I'll see what I can do."

Cody smirked and the conversation moved on to more mundane topics. For the first time since seeing Barrera in Devon's home, Jane felt like she could breathe a little easier.

CHAPTER THIRTEEN

"I MUST SAY, THAT WAS A COMMANDING PERFORMANCE."
Cody watched the amber liquid swirl as he played with his glass.
"One might think you were actually falling for her."

"You know," Devon looked up from his game of billiards to eye
his friend. "Some people find your brand of humor amusing. I don't."

"I guess my concern is this," Cody ignored the barb. "You and I
both know that you aren't a forever kind of guy, but does Jane?
Because she strikes me as a forever kind of girl."

"And this is your business how?"

"I like her. I'd hate to see her get hurt."

As much as Devon agreed, as much as he knew he should stay
well away from Jane Russell rather than break her heart, it pissed
him off to no end to hear it come from Cody. He placed his cue on
the table and straightened to look the senator in the eye. "Let me get
this straight: The most talented womanizer I know is warning me
about hurting a woman. Hello, hypocrisy."

"Nah," Cody let the words roll right off him, choosing to instead
pick up Devon's cue to take the shot he'd left behind. "It's not so
much hypocrisy as a 'learn from my mistakes' kind of thing. You
think you're in purgatory now, wait until you've hurt her and she
can't even say your name without snarling a little. That's true hell."

Cody's ominous warning hovered in Devon's mind the rest of
the night. He tucked his toothbrush into the medicine cabinet and

stopped to stare at his reflection in the mirror. Was he being selfish by not showing more self-control where Jane was concerned? He couldn't begin to explain his actions; he'd never in his life been unable to control himself like this.

Even now, when he had so much hanging in the balance and hours of work to be done, he found himself fighting the urge to gather a sampling of all his favorite roses, take them to her room and make her a bed out of their silken petals. Then he'd lay her down in the middle of those petals....

Devon splashed cold water on his face and shook his head like a dog. Allowing his thoughts to continue down that path wouldn't do anybody any good. Instead, he looked over the latest reports from his security team. The royal bodyguards would be arriving in the morning to do a sweep before Aolani arrived. He wanted to be certain everything was ready before then.

Not that one could ever feel truly ready for royalty to be a houseguest. When he was with Alex and her family, there was such an easy camaraderie that he usually forgot who his new niece was. Every now and then, though, it would hit him that the loveable teen was actually the ruler of a small country. It was stranger still to think that his little sister had married into royalty and was now acting as a surrogate mother to the young queen. Between assuming the role of guardian to Lani and now having infant twins, Alex had definitely plunged into motherhood head first.

It was hard for Devon to go to sleep that night; he was too excited about his family visiting and too flummoxed over Jane. The combination made sleep more elusive than it had been on Christmas Eve as a child. In a moment of rare weakness, he allowed his mind to drift back to a time when they'd still been a whole family, before Victoria McAlister had decided to leave them to pursue her own path – a path that didn't include being their mom.

There was a lot of laughter then. Victoria was like a ray of sunshine whenever she entered a room; her smile was contagious. Her laughter could inspire even her stoic husband to be impetuous. It was a time Devon didn't often visit, though. It left him too raw. Memories of her always led to memories of watching her go.

Every so often, he would hear rumors of her whereabouts. Sometimes she was on a grand adventure. Sometimes she was in a mental hospital somewhere. She was never headed home, though. He'd been a preteen when he'd read in a tabloid that he had another little sister. His mother had met a man in Ecuador while painting in the jungle. Of course, she also left the little girl just as she had her first family. Devon couldn't get the thought of his second sister out of his mind, though. As soon as he was old enough, he'd gone to Ecuador to find her.

At first, Karise had wanted nothing to do with the McAlisters. It had taken Devon many years and many trips to convince her to allow him to help with even her college. Over those trips, he'd fallen in love with this country, these people. Sometimes he felt spread too thin, trying to maintain the McAlister legacy while forging his own, but it was worth it. This place was his paradise, and these people were more his kin than any he'd ever known.

When he'd started his plantation, it was Karise's father who'd helped him find the land. The entire family had gone out of their way to help him get his feet on the ground. To this day, Pablo was his most trusted friend and ally. Devon's mother had broken many hearts along her journey, but Devon was oddly glad for what she'd done because it had led him here.

It was well into the night before Devon drifted off to sleep and well before dawn when his eyes opened again. Rather than waste more time lying in bed with his brain on overload, he decided to go check on the cubs before starting his day. They had such a calming effect on Jane; maybe they'd do the same for him. He slid on a pair of jeans and didn't even bother buttoning his shirt before heading down to the stables.

It was still quiet when he got there. Horses nickered at him from their stalls. He stopped to say hello to each of the magnificent Andalusians, wondering when he'd last spent time with them, let alone ridden. By the time he made it to the stall housing the cubs, they were awake and protesting their hunger.

After much fumbling, he found the milk Maria had set aside for them and made two bottles. The visit wasn't turning out to be nearly as relaxing as he'd hoped. He sat in the straw with his back against the wall and was instantly overrun by hungry jaguar cubs. He didn't have the faintest clue how to manage both bottles at the same time. It took some maneuvering, but their frantic scuffle for the best bottle calmed, and both were finally happy. Settled peacefully, Devon rested his head against the wall and watched the kittens with a small smile.

That was the last thing he remembered before dozing off. He awoke to Jane's gentle fingers brushing his cheek. In a sleepy fog, he thought about kissing her, but she'd already taken Aria from his lap and slid down the wall to sit beside him. She rested her head on his shoulder without a word, and he found himself unable to resist the heavy pull of slumber.

"Just wait until your sister hears about this."

Devon's eyes flew open at the sound of his brother-in-law's highly amused voice. It took him a second to process where he was and what was happening. The sun was now well into its ascent. Devon could hear stable hands going about their day. Next to him, Jane was rousing.

"I should have known you'd come with the early security team." Devon stretched his back before putting the black jaguar cub down in the straw beside him so he could stand. He brushed the straw off him before shaking Daniel Martin's hand. "It's good to see you again, Daniel. I hope life is treating you well."

Everything in Daniel's expression said he wanted to ask what was going on. He showed more discretion than his wife would have, had she been there. "Things are great. And you?"

"It's been a bit of a crazy week, but things are good. We have a lot to catch up on." Devon reached out an arm to pull Jane to his side now that she was standing as well. He knew the act wouldn't be lost on Daniel, and he'd probably hear about it from Alex later, but he couldn't stop himself from making the possessive gesture. "Daniel, this is Jane Russell. Jane, this is my brother-in-law, Daniel Martin."

"I'm so happy to meet you. I've heard such good things about your family." Jane's voice was soft and lilting as she extended a hand.

"It's a pleasure to meet you, too. I'm looking forward to hearing more about you." Daniel's eyes went from Jane to Devon and back again. "I hope I'm not interrupting anything."

"Not at all," Jane was quick to assure him. "We've been taking care of these orphaned cubs, so sleep is a rare commodity. But then, I guess you know all about that with your twins."

Daniel smiled warmly at Jane. "That I do. There's never a moment's rest."

"This is Aria." Jane held the cub toward Daniel for him to see. When he reached out to scratch her ears, Aria hissed. "Sorry. She'll warm up to you. The little black one is Freya. They're my babies. Not quite the same, but just as good at depriving me of sleep."

"She's very cute, and a good judge of character," Daniel quipped.

Devon did his best not to grin like a schoolboy at them. It made him happy to see the two of them get along so well, though. He was suddenly very eager to introduce Jane to Alex.

"Why don't I ask Lucia to whip up some breakfast while Jane and I clean up? I'll leave you with the latest reports from my chief of security, and then we can go over some of the finer details over breakfast," Devon suggested.

The trio chatted easily as they made their way back to the house. Devon couldn't take his eyes off Jane the entire way. She looked delectable in her pajamas with her hair spilling out of the loose braid she'd slept in. He was loath to let go of her hand when they parted ways at the top of the stairs.

He found himself whistling as he readied for the day and almost bounding down the stairs in his exuberance. He and Daniel were the first to arrive in the dining room. Lucia had already begun to set breakfast out. The aroma of waffles made his stomach rumble.

Daniel looked up from the stack of papers he'd been sifting through, his expression serious. "You've really stumbled into it this time, haven't you, Devon?"

"There was no way to contact you to tell you to cancel the trip without letting Barrera realize we knew what was going on. Cody seems to think we're safe as long as we don't poke the hornet's nest."

"So you're just going to let them take her jaguar preserve?"

"Hell, no. We're just waiting to reclaim it until you and your family have gone home." Devon's response was swift. "The adult jaguars that roam the bulk of the preserve are most likely safe for the time being. Jane has the cubs with her, and their mother was killed.

Cody says this gives him time to bring in a team qualified to handle the situation."

"Do I want to know why or how he has access to such a team?"

"Probably not. I've learned the less I know about the U.S. government, the safer I feel." Devon glanced either way to be sure Lucia wasn't around before stealing a piece of bacon from the plate she'd just set on the table.

"It's sad how true that is."

"If you want to cancel the trip, I understand."

Daniel swiped his own piece of bacon before responding. "No. Cody's right. If we cancel, they'll know something's up. Besides, Hezbollah is like a cancer spreading across the globe faster than even most governments realize. At least I know where they are here, so I know which direction to watch."

"How do you do it? How do you watch over your family without being completely riddled with ulcers? This past week has been nerve-wracking." Devon ran his fingers through his hair in frustration.

"Who says I'm not riddled with ulcers? Your sister is a particularly headstrong woman. She's always getting herself into some fray or another."

"True," Devon acknowledged. Keeping up with her had been a full-time job. She was also a strong woman who really didn't need to be protected, truth be told, but as her big brother he'd felt duty-bound to try – when she'd let him.

"So, uh, Jane." Daniel grinned.

Devon couldn't help matching with a smile of his own. "She's pretty fantastic, isn't she?"

"That right there is the real reason I can't cancel," Daniel chuckled. "Alex would kill me if she missed seeing that look on your face."

CHAPTER FOURTEEN

JANE WANTED TO THROW UP. Her nerves danced with anticipation as she watched the procession of expensive cars bumping along the winding drive that led to the main house. She'd tried to hang back with Aldo and Maria, to let family greet family, but Devon insisted she stay close to his side.

Oddly enough, Jane remembered seeing pictures of Alexandra Martin once, back when she was still Alexandra McAlister. Jane had been standing in line at Edwards Grocery, and she couldn't help scanning the headlines of the gossip rags. It was a crazy thing to remember, but Jane distinctly recalled feeling both sorry for Alex's complete lack of privacy and appalled at her complete lack of morals. The daughter of a well-known corporate mogul, the girl's exploits had the paparazzi in a constant feeding frenzy.

Now, Jane was absolutely ill in the face of meeting a woman who was not only incomparably beautiful, but deeply important to Devon. As Alex unfolded herself from the middle sedan, Jane had only a moment to be impressed with how put together she was despite her long travel before Daniel was sweeping her into his arms. Jane tried to remember how long the pair had been married even as she felt a small stab of jealousy over how obviously in love they were.

Someone from inside the car handed an infant out to Alex, who passed the child along to Daniel before claiming a second infant from the hands in the car. The teenage girl who climbed out next was both stunning and regally graceful, despite the casual jeans and faded T-shirt she wore. Jane glanced at Devon for direction, wondering if she was expected to bow.

"Crazy, isn't it?" Devon whispered against Jane's ear. A shiver ran the length of her spine. She swallowed hard before nodding in agreement. He continued on, seemingly oblivious to her physical response. "Sometimes she almost seems like a normal teenager, but she's technically the queen now. I keep forgetting that, even though I went to her coronation."

"I can't fathom having that much responsibility at that young of an age," Jane muttered. At 16, her biggest concern was convincing her cousin Charlie not to tell her folks he'd caught her making out with Jimmy Montgomery in the back row of the movie theater.

"Come on. I want you to meet everybody." Devon wrapped his arm tighter around her and pulled Jane along with him.

His behavior had Jane completely off kilter. All day, he'd been acting like he was introducing his girlfriend to family. She had no clue what she was supposed to make of his actions, since their last discussion on the topic had ended with the same consensus as always: Devon and Jane were looking for very different things in life.

"Holy crap. He has a girl with him."

Those were the first words Jane heard from Devon's little sister. Daniel and Devon both gave her a look – one amused, one irritated. Alex clapped a hand over her mouth. Aolani stifled a giggle.

"That was so rude of me. I'm sorry. That was shock speaking. Devon has never invited a woman to his home before."

"It's okay. My filter breaks down more times than I care to count." Jane recovered quickly, filing away that little bit of information for later as she extended a hand to Alex. "I'm Jane Russell. I work on the jaguar preserve next door to Devon. He was kind enough to let my colleagues and me stay here after our fire."

Alex shook Jane's hand, waved in acknowledgement at Maria and Aldo, then gave her brother a searching look before turning back to Jane. "It's good to meet you, Jane. Really good."

"Lucky for you, *mi princesa*, I'm too happy to see you to be angry." Devon let go of Jane long enough to wrap Alex and the baby she held in a hug. "You look amazing, my dear."

"You look happy." Alex wrapped her free arm around Devon. "I missed you."

"I've missed you, too." His voice was low, but Jane heard it. There was such tenderness and adoration in his tone; it made Jane's heart trip a funny little beat.

After extracting herself from her brother's arms, Alex looked around expectantly, confusion falling across her face after she didn't find what she was looking for. "Where's Cass?"

"On a vacation." Devon gave half the answer.

"Good for her." Alex nodded approvingly. Jane wondered if she'd still feel that way after she got the other half of the answer, or if she'd be mad at Jane for driving a wedge between Devon and his best employee.

Next thing Jane new, everyone was talking at once. There were hugs going all around. Devon hugged his teenage niece, introducing her to Jane as Lani before inspecting his five-month-old niece and nephew. The new arrivals were introduced to Maria and Aldo. Cody made his appearance, triggering another round of hugs. All this happened amidst happy chatter that floated around Jane.

She soaked it all in, seeing a whole new side to Devon. He pretended to bite his nephew's stomach, eliciting a delighted laugh from the baby, who grabbed Devon by the nose and refused to let go.

"Have you officially met Joseph yet?" Devon tried to pull the child off his nose with no success.

"I have not. He's very cute." Jane forced a smile, her eyes searching for something else in the room to focus on – anything besides the little boy who looked startlingly like his uncle. Jane had never considered herself a baby-crazy kind of woman. She'd babysat as a teenager and liked kids well enough, but since she'd found out she wouldn't have children of her own, she'd found it didn't hurt as much if she limited her exposure to other people's offspring. Still, she could usually be around mini people without making a fool of herself. But there was something about this charming child with his wide grin, dimples, and sparkling brown eyes that made an intense pain shoot through her heart.

"Do you want to hold Erena?" Alex rose from her spot on the couch to hold the little girl out toward Jane.

Jane shoved her hands in her pockets rather than give in to the itch to reach out and touch the baby's angelically soft skin. The girl looked up at Jane with big toffee-colored eyes to match those of her brother, mother, and uncle. Jane caught a glimpse of two white teeth when Erena smiled at her. Certain her own smile was lame, she did her best to brighten her countenance. "I'd love to, but I have to go check on my jaguar cubs. You have a beautiful family, Alex. I can see why Devon adores you all."

Without waiting for a reply, Jane made her escape. She wondered if Devon would explain her odd behavior to his sister. Part of her was horrified at the prospect. Another part of her hoped he would so the other woman didn't think she was a total lunatic. All she really knew was that the back of her throat was burning with the need to cry, and she had to get herself together before dinner.

After checking in quickly on Aria and Freya, Jane made her way up the back stairway to her room unnoticed. There, she allowed the tears to fall. It seemed colossally unfair that she be precluded from the motherhood club. Why had she been selected among women to never know what it felt like to have a child move inside her? For the first time, she was overcome with grief that she'd never look at another human being and see her own face reflected.

Jane had always tried to take the trials of life in stride. She didn't usually question God, trusting that His love was big enough for even the things she couldn't understand. But in that moment of raw pain, she was struggling to understand what possible good could come of her tattered fallopian tubes. She was struggling to trust. And in that moment, all she really wanted was to feel Devon's arms around her, to hear him say he wanted her, damaged reproductive organs and all.

Jane nearly cried herself to sleep. She didn't know how long she lay there, somewhere between slumber and waking, her mind numb. When the shadows on the wall changed length, she knew it was time to pull herself together again. By the time she was seated to Devon's right, directly across from Alex and beside Cody, she was freshly scrubbed and feeling almost human again.

She began the evening with a polite smile and small talk, but as dinner progressed she felt herself loosening up enough to truly enjoy her companions. Devon was being absurdly attentive, and she couldn't help flushing with pleasure under his adoring gaze.

Alex seemed genuinely interested in Jane, her jaguars, and her family. Although Alex was easy to talk to and Jane didn't mind sharing, she was much more interested in hearing Alex's stories. Devon's sister was startlingly intelligent. Her quick wit was most evident when she verbally sparred with her husband, an activity both obviously enjoyed.

"So let me get this straight." Jane stopped eating to look at Alex incredulously. "You first met Lani when you saved her from an assassination attempt, and the first time you saw Daniel, he held a gun to your head because he thought you were the assassin?"

"Not exactly. The first time I saw Daniel, he was trying to bully me into letting him mine my volcano for diamonds," Alex clarified before attempting to feed Joseph a spoonful of mashed bananas.

"Excuse me. I was not bullying you and it was not *your* mountain. You have such a revisionist memory," Daniel argued, wiping his forehead to remove the bananas Erena had flung at him. The baby dug her fingers into the bowl in front of her, squealing with glee when another glob of fruit flew at her dad.

"I told you not to give her the bowl." Alex arched her eyebrows knowingly before turning back to Joseph.

"Either way, it was a rather inauspicious beginning," Devon interjected before the two could escalate either conversation to a battle. "But they worked together to save Lani and the rest is history."

"I'll tell you the rest when Daniel isn't around to interrupt," Alex promised.

"It's a good thing you're pretty." Daniel sighed.

Devon took over the conversation. "So, how long can you stay with us, Cody?"

"I'll take off about the time the Martins leave, maybe a day earlier if everything seems quiet. I have a meeting back at the ranch before I head to D.C. It'll take my associate a couple of days to get here after he's briefed. Just hunker down and don't make any waves, and I think you'll be fine, though."

"That's reassuring," Jane muttered.

"Should you stay behind with some of our security detail to help cover the gap, Daniel?" Alex frowned.

Devon gave his sister a bemused look. "As much as I appreciate you offering to loan me your husband as protection, I'm sure we'll be fine."

"Did that bruise your manly ego, sweetie?" Alex made a face at him.

"Just a bit, yeah." Devon reached around to tug her ponytail playfully.

"Well, go smoke a cigar and drink some Scotch to see if you can recover it. I'll see if I can sweet talk one of these lovely ladies into helping me bathe the twins."

"I have a Web chat scheduled with a friend." Lani was quick to excuse herself from the duty.

"Five bucks says that friend is Aaron Johnston," Alex leaned over to whisper to Jane. "Her royal highness is crazy about a Missouri farm boy. Talk about star-crossed young love."

"I don't know if that's sweet or sad." Jane furrowed her brow.

"Both," Alex answered.

"I'll take care of the cubs," Maria offered, giving Jane a pointed look. "You go help Alex."

Jane knew to protest would be rude, so she smiled at Alex and said she'd be glad to assist. Her years of babysitting came flooding back, and she easily stepped into the role of caregiver. Other than to smile or play with a baby, neither uttered a word for the first ten minutes as they worked side by side. Alex was the first to speak.

"You're obviously good with children." She paused mid-sentence to eye Jane curiously. "Why didn't you want to hold Erena earlier? If that's too personal a question, just tell me to mind my own business."

Jane laughed softly at Alex's refreshing candor. "I don't mind. A few years ago, I had a really bad bought of appendicitis. I stupidly refused to go to the doctor when my stomach first started hurting. By the time I was in enough pain to get help, things were pretty bad. I found out after the surgery that it actually damaged my reproductive organs, so I can't have children."

"I'm so sorry." Alex surprised Jane by giving her a one-armed hug, made even more awkward by the infant each of them held. "That's horrible. Are they positive?"

Jane nodded. "I went to three different doctors. My fiancé was adamant that we be certain."

"Your fiancé?"

"We called the wedding off." Jane shrugged lightly, focusing intently on rinsing the soap off Erena. "It wasn't meant to be."

Alex's brow furrowed, but she didn't speak.

"Most days I don't even think about it. Honestly, I was pretty content with my jaguars. It didn't bother me for a long time."

"What changed?"

"I don't know. Probably something about your beautiful children just made me wonder what it would be like if things were different."

"Something," Alex mused.

"You're fishing to hear that it was your brother who changed things."

"Not at all."

Jane smirked, not believing Alex for one second. "Maybe he has had the tiniest impact on it."

"I'm guessing you've heard he's a playboy," Alex said abruptly.

"Indigenous tribes with no modern technologies have heard he's a playboy."

A snort of laughter escaped Alex before she turned it into a more sedate chuckle. "I like you."

"Thank you."

"Because I like you, I'm going to be a bad sister and meddle. We had a pretty suckish mom. I think it's made Devon a little gun-shy when it comes to trusting women. My personal theory is that he's always gravitated to women who couldn't break his heart. He's not a bad guy, though. And I think he really cares about you. No, I take that back. I know he adores you. You're different. I can see it all over his face."

Jane wasn't sure how to respond to most of what Alex had just said. She stuck with the one subject she did have a response for. "He told me about your mom. I'm sorry."

"He told you about Victoria? It must be love. He doesn't talk to *me* about her."

"You really think so?"

Alex handed Jane a newly diapered Joseph, taking a naked Erena from her before responding. "You'll have to talk to him about that, but yeah, I think it says a lot about his feelings for you."

"He named a rose after me," Jane admitted.

"Seriously? I want a rose named after me."

The conversation moved on after that. Alex listened intently as Jane talked about the jaguar reintroduction program she'd been working on. Jane soaked up every word Alex said when it came to rare earth minerals and how McAlister Industries had begun to harvest them for safer, more environmentally friendly technologies. The two women chatted continuously through the entire process of getting the babies into bed, lowering their voices when it came time to tuck the little ones in.

They resumed their conversation full force as they made their way down the stairs to join the men and Maria on the patio for drinks. Jane could feel Devon's eyes on her the moment she stepped outside. There was a look in them that made her feel like a delicious dessert, and that sent a thrill of pleasure racing down her spine.

Devon rose to greet them. "I don't know if I'm terrified or delighted to see the two of you getting along so well."

"I'd forgotten your sister was a scientist. It's nice to be around someone who speaks the same language I do." Jane smiled at Alex before accepting Devon's outstretched hand.

"What language is that – dork?" Daniel's smart-aleck grin told Jane his words were meant to goad his wife.

"It's a better language than grunt," Alex quipped.

"Have I told you how amazing you look tonight?" Devon murmured against Jane's ear. "Because if I haven't, it was terribly remiss of me."

"I suppose I forgive you." Jane realized it was effortless to stop thinking about all the reasons she shouldn't lean back into Devon and simply enjoy being in his embrace, her back against his solid chest, his arms wrapped around her. Something about it felt incredibly right – beyond the thrill of desire it ignited.

The evening was enchanting. The company, the laughter, and Devon's constant touch did as much to intoxicate Jane as the wine she swirled in her glass. By the time she bid Devon a lingering goodnight at the top of the stairs, she was lightheaded.

Jane hummed happily to herself as she went to change into her pajamas, or rather, an old pair of Alex's pajamas. When she entered the closet looking for something to wear, she stopped short at the neat pile of clothing boxes with a note on top: "I thought you might like something of your own to wear."

Jane recognized Devon's distinctive script. Her heart sped up as she fumbled with the first box, her fingers inexplicably clumsy. Inside she found a dusty rose- and cream-colored pajama set. Jane ran her fingers lovingly over the satin and lace camisole and matching shorts. Without waiting to see what was in the other boxes, she changed into the first gift. She felt so pretty in the delicate clothing; it made her glad she'd taken the time to shave her legs before dinner.

Once ready for bed, she returned to the boxes in the closet and sat on the plush rug to open the next treasure. First was a robe to match her pajamas. Next were shirts, jeans, and shorts. Then a swimsuit followed by two dresses. The second to last box was full of bras, panties, and socks. The grand finale was a new pair of hiking boots. Jane was in awe at his kind gesture. She wondered how he'd managed to find her a complete wardrobe out here on the edge of the jungle. He must have had someone deliver it to her room for him while they were at dinner.

The temptation to seek him out was more than she could bear. He'd been so attentive lately, so caring. That combined with her undeniable attraction to him on the basest of levels to make him irresistible. The devil on her shoulder said it was only polite to find him and thank him, right away. If that led to something more, then so be it. The angel that sat on the other shoulder reminded her she would most likely regret her actions in the harsh light of day, when reality sank in.

But morning felt really far away. With a groan, she fell back onto her bed, tossing one arm across her eyes and willing herself to think of something else. Anything else. But the only thing that came to mind was Devon's smiling eyes, that rakish grin of his, and the way his hands had felt flat against her stomach when he'd pulled her up against him that night on the patio.

A tap at the door broke her reverie. She scurried off the bed, wrapping the robe around her as she crossed the room.

Devon looked nervous standing in her doorway. Maybe not nervous so much as distracted. Jane couldn't quite read the look in his eyes as he spoke. "You got the clothes. Good. Do you like them?"

"I love them," Jane assured him. "I was just debating if it was too late to come find you to say thank you. You didn't have to do this, though. It's too much. I was okay with your sister's clothes."

"I was happy to do it." He waved off her protest. "Maria helped me out, though. I made arrangements with a store in Quito. She and Aldo took an overnight trip to go pick them up and get some new things for themselves while they were at it."

Jane frowned. Had she really been so wrapped up in herself that she hadn't noticed them gone?

"What's wrong? Don't you like the clothes?"

"I can't believe I didn't notice they'd left."

"There's been a lot going on. I was personally kind of glad they weren't around when Barrera made his appearance. Aldo might have shot him, and then all hell would have broken loose."

Jane nodded, not fully letting herself off the hook. She blamed her inattention less on the chaos of the week and more on how fully Devon saturated her thoughts and senses.

"I'll, uh, I'll let you get back to whatever you were doing. I don't mean to keep you."

He turned to go. Everything in Jane screamed not to let him leave.

"Devon?" Her voice sounded pathetic in her own ears.

He turned back toward her.

"I was actually just thinking about finding you so I could do this…."

Jane grabbed Devon and pulled him to her, standing on tiptoe so she could kiss him. It was the first time in her life she had initiated a touch, but now that she'd committed to the bold act she gave it all she had. In that moment, more than she needed air, she needed him to kiss her back as hungrily as she was clinging to him.

Something akin to a growl rumbled low in his throat, and with it his restraint snapped. Jane found herself in his arms, her legs wrapped around his hips as he moved them back into her room, kicking the door closed behind him. With one arm, she clung to his broad shoulders. Her free hand found its way to his thick, dark hair.

Her blond curls spilled around them, veiling them both as she tilted her head down to meet his ravenous mouth.

He eased her back onto the bed, freeing his hands to explore her gentle curves, his large hands splayed out, running along her ribs to the small of her waist and across her flat belly, then back up to the swell of her breasts. Jane arched into him, greedily seeking more of his touch, her own hands tugging at his shirt so she could feel his skin on hers.

He pulled away long enough to tug the shirt over his head before returning to her. She trembled with the need to experience more of him. Never in her life had she felt more cherished than she did when his lips reclaimed hers. This time his touch held more reverence than hunger.

The last vestiges of Jane's defenses crumbled. She opened herself up to be wholly and completely his. Everything blended into a beautiful symphony of emotions, of desire. Touching, being touched. Clothes found their way to the floor. Skin on skin, Jane never wanted to stop caressing, clinging, exploring, yet the intensity building from the heat and friction between them made her wonder how much more she could take.

She was on the verge of pleading with him to end her sweet torment when something inside her snapped. With a little growl of her own, she rolled him over and began an assault on his senses. It was her turn to take him to the edge of reason and beyond.

When they finally found release, Jane was certain she'd drown in the onslaught of sensation. With a soft cry, she pulled him up, clutching him to her, her head buried in his shoulder so he wouldn't see the tears roll down her cheeks. Whether he'd seen them or merely sensed them, Devon cradled her gently in his lap, stroking her hair and whispering words of her beauty.

It was the words that were missing that made Jane cry all the harder.

CHAPTER
FIFTEEN

JANE HAD BEEN RIGHT; there was a difference. Never had Devon been so profoundly moved or forever changed by another's touch. He hadn't known it possible. Now that he did, it terrified him. Her tears on his shoulder told him she'd been every bit as affected by the encounter—and that scared him even more.

Devon didn't know what to do next, another in the long line of new feelings Jane brought with her. Regardless of his current confusion, he wasn't ready to break the spell between them. He shifted them both so he could lie down with her wrapped safely in his arms. He stroked her hair, wondering if he'd ever stop being fascinated by her and wishing there was something he could do to make her feel better.

Understanding the source of her tears would probably be a good start, he knew, but he didn't have the courage to ask. He wasn't entirely certain he wanted to know the answer. Was she merely as affected as he, or was there something else amiss? He didn't think he could bear the guilt if she regretted what had happened between them. Jane was everything light and good in the world. He didn't want to be the one to tarnish that glow. Had he already?

Jane grew quiet; her breath evened. Devon debated going back to his own room but quickly set the notion aside. He couldn't bring himself to let go of her yet. He didn't know how long it took her to fall asleep or what time it was when he finally drifted off as well. He couldn't have slept long, though, because it was still before dawn when he sensed she was awake and his eyes flew open.

She was propped up on one elbow, studying him with solemn green eyes. Devon wanted to take her delicate face in his hands, to pepper her sweet nose and cheeks with kisses. The look in her eyes stilled his hand, though. It was Jane who reached out to place a hand on Devon's cheek; he instinctively leaned into the touch.

"You are such a beautiful man," she murmured, never taking her eyes off him.

He captured her hand, bringing it to his lips to brush a kiss against her palm.

There was a hint of sadness to her smile. "You've always been honest about who you are. I don't want you to worry that I'll expect something more from you."

Devon furrowed his brow, not entirely following her.

"I can feel you pulling away from me." She stopped as if searching for the words that should come next. With a mirthless laugh, she continued. "I guess I just don't want you to worry that I'll be expecting a ring or anything. You don't have to start preparing an exit strategy. I'm a big girl. I made my choice, eyes open."

"Ah." Devon wasn't sure how to respond to that. She was giving him a free pass. He could read in her body language that it wasn't what she wanted. He knew she was being the bigger person, and if ever there was a time to reassure her he had no intentions of going anywhere, this was it.

But the right words just wouldn't form. Instead of saying any of the things tumbling around inside him, he found himself telling her she was a remarkable woman who never ceased to amaze him. He could see in her eyes it wasn't the answer she hoped to hear, but it was the only response he could give. The weight of her disappointment was crushing.

"I guess I'd better go or we'll never hear the end of it from my sister."

"Or Cody. I think he's almost as bad as she is," Jane added. She leaned down to kiss him. Her touch was soft as an angel's wing. He didn't intend to deepen the kiss, yet somehow he did. His hands were reaching out for her. Something inside him said to never let her go.

She placed her hands flat on his chest, stopping him from pulling her closer. He considered persuading her otherwise.

"If you're going to leave, you'd better go." There was no malice in her words, no accusation. That didn't stop him from feeling like the world's biggest ass when he got out of that bed, though. He gathered his clothes, ignoring the voice in his head that told him to return to her while he could. But he didn't stop, not even when he thought he heard her crying after he closed the door.

It was the sound of those tears that haunted him as he went through his morning routine. By the time he sat down to eat his breakfast alone in the kitchen, he was as surly as a bear with a thorn in his paw. Naturally, that didn't dissuade his sister from making herself comfortable on the stool next to him when she stumbled in looking for some coffee.

"So I hear Lucia is after you to get into the coffee business."

For once, Devon wished his sister would go away. He wanted to be alone with his misery. "I'm not sure I'm ready to add anything new to my plate at the moment."

"If you wanted to add Jane to your plate, I wouldn't complain. I like her." She smiled slyly at him.

"Of course you went there."

Alex straightened and frowned. "What's that supposed to mean?"

"Just that you naturally gravitated to the one subject I hoped you'd steer clear of this morning. Hell, it's the reason I tried to eat breakfast alone."

"I just asked about coffee."

"No, you asked about coffee then tried to stick your nose in my love life."

Alex arched an eyebrow, pinning him with her haughtiest glare. "Gee, I'm sorry I got a little excited that my middle-aged brother finally has something resembling a mature love life."

"I'm not middle-aged."

Alex snorted.

"That was ladylike."

"You're old enough to at least pretend to be an adult," she rejoined.

"Let me get this straight. Running two multinational corporations doesn't qualify me as an adult; it's having a little woman at home that officially makes me a man?" Devon was so angry, little red dots danced in his vision.

"This one would and you know it. I think that's why you're scared."

"I'm not scared."

"Bull. And I help with McAlister."

It was Devon's turn to pin Alex with a haughty glare. "When's the last board meeting you attended?"

"You know I hate board meetings. They're your talent, not mine."

"That's your excuse? I think you can do better."

Alex rose menacingly from her chair, making Devon suspect she was getting ready to fly into him. "So now you're going to deflect the 'I'm not man enough to admit I'm in love' conversation by attacking me for not attending board meetings? That's really where you want to take this?"

"I'm not attacking anyone! I just wanted to eat my frigging toast in peace. Was there anything about my countenance this morning that said 'talk to me'?"

She slammed her hand down on the counter. "You are such a flipping coward. You used to be my hero, you know that?"

"But then what, you grew up?" Devon's voice was cold.

Alex sighed, her voice softening. "Maybe. Or maybe you just didn't. Jane isn't Victoria."

"What's that supposed to mean?"

"Why am I even bothering with you? You're not going to listen. You're such a smart man – you figure it out. After all, you do run two corporations."

Alex's scowl could have melted iron. She swiped her coffee off the counter and stormed out of the room, but not before tossing over her shoulder that the coffee was good and he should listen to Lucia.

If Devon's mood had been sour before, it was downright formidable now. A very guttural part of him wanted to pay a visit to Javier. Maybe if he beat Barrera to a pulp, Devon would feel better about life and Jane could get her jaguar preserve back. The logical part of him won out, and he opted for attacking his workload instead.

The longer he spent in the office, the more woefully obvious it was that he desperately needed Cass around to even have a prayer of staying on top of his work. While she was on his mind, he sent her a quick email saying he hoped she was well and enjoying her vacation. Once he had the worst of the fires put out, he went to look for Maria. While sifting through email, it had occurred to him that she'd been the preserve's office manager. Maybe she'd be willing to help him at least keep his head above water until she could get back to her usual job.

When he could no longer reasonably avoid it without admitting cowardice, he went looking for his sister. Daniel found him first. One look at his brother-in-law's face told him Alex had not kept their fight between them.

"Do you remember once telling me not to hurt your little sister?" Daniel wasted no time getting to the point.

"I know, I know. I'm looking for her so I can apologize."

"You made her cry, Devon. She hates crying. I hate watching her cry."

"I already feel like an ass. Just tell me where she is and I'll try to fix it."

"She and Lani are at the waterfall. I was just getting the twins settled in with Pablo and Lucia before meeting them. Want to walk with me?"

"Are you finished with the guilt trip?"

"I think so. No promises, though. It feels kind of good to be on this end of things for a change."

"Glad I could help." Devon fell in step beside Daniel. Despite Daniel's ribbing, the walk to the little waterfall that made Devon's favorite swimming hole was a peaceful one. Unlike the cliff Devon and Jane had plunged off of not so long ago, this smaller waterfall was gentle enough to play in. The water it fed was relatively predator-free. On the rare occasion Devon found time to visit it, he always left in a better mood.

He decided today might be the exception to that rule when he realized Daniel had neglected to mention that Jane was with the swimming party. The black two-piece he'd bought her looked every bit as delectable on her as he'd imagined it would. With her damp hair tumbling down her back and water glistening on her alabaster skin, she looked like a goddess to him. Devon's throat constricted. He fought the urge to run and hide.

"Did I forget to mention Jane was here?" Daniel asked with feigned innocence. "Whoops."

Devon shot him a glare that would have made a lesser man crumble.

Daniel ignored it. "Believe it or not, I do feel your pain, brother. I put up one hell of a fight when it came to falling for your sister. At the time, I was certain it just had to be that way."

Never taking his eyes off Jane, Devon nodded slowly. As she approached, her gaze caught his. He wished he could read her expression.

"You know the crazy thing?" Daniel continued. "I can't for the life of me even remember my reasons for fighting. And I can't begin to imagine my life without her."

Devon cast a glance Daniel's way. He appreciated his friend's words; he just didn't know what to say in return. But, as is often the case between friends, Daniel didn't need a reply. He clapped Devon on the shoulder before turning his attention to his wife and the teen they both considered a daughter.

After waving at the women in the water, Devon kicked off his shoes and rolled up his jeans so he could sit on a rock and dangle his feet in the pool. He imagined coming back, just him and Jane, to swim naked in the moonlight. That led to memories of the night before. If he thought hard enough, he could still taste her sweetness on his lips; he could feel her warm and alive and brimming with love in his arms.

As if to punctuate his torment, Jane's laughter drifted on a breeze. He couldn't help smiling in response to her smile. The last thing he ever wanted to do was hurt her. Yet before their relationship was even truly begun, he'd done just that. He had to admit to himself that "relationship" probably wasn't the right word. She'd been a fascination to him and at times even an obsession. He wasn't entirely sure he was able to claim anything more, though.

Alex made her way over to Devon, wringing her wet hair out on him before sitting down and leaning against his side.

"I suppose you drenching me is my penance for this morning?" Devon commented ruefully.

"You're not even close to paying for this morning," Alex countered.

"Figures. So none of my previous good deeds help balance out the ledger? What about that time I saved your life?" Teasing Alex was easier than voicing the truth.

"It might count for something if you would tell me what's really going on."

Devon cut his eyes toward his sister then back at Jane. "I don't know if I'm ready to sort out what's going on in my head right now, and I for damned sure don't want to start talking feelings. Can we please just enjoy this visit, though, and not try to find all of the answers to my love life, or lack thereof, according to you?"

"As long as you don't bite my head off again," Alex stipulated. "And as long as you understand that I really, really like Jane and I plan to invite her to things. Can you be around her without being a total grouse?"

"I'll do my very best-est," he promised with mock solemnity.

"You're joking, but I really will kick your ass if you do that again. Don't yell at me. I don't like it."

"For someone who doesn't like yelling, you sure do a lot of it."

Alex's response was to shove him into the water. Devon came up sputtering and shaking his head like a wet dog. He slapped the water, sending a retaliatory spray of water her direction, but it had less effect since she was already wet and in a swimsuit.

"You're buying me a new phone. This is the second swim this phone has taken in as many weeks."

"You're just saying that because you don't know how to order a phone," Alex retorted. "You are so lost without Cassandra."

Devon scowled. There was no debating the truth of her words – yet another reason for him to part ways with Jane. Even as he thought it, he knew things would never go back to normal with Cassandra. Now that he knew the true nature of her feelings for him, it was going to be virtually impossible for them to work side by side as they'd done in the past. Only he had no idea what the fair solution was to that particular mystery.

Deciding to take an "if you can't beat them, join them" approach, he stripped his shirt off and tossed it on the bank before fishing his drenched phone out of his pocket and tossing it up to Alex. Then he sank back beneath the surface, willing the cool water to wash away his worries. It didn't work.

He went through the motions of joining in the playful banter at the pool, keeping a careful distance from Jane lest he yield to the temptation to pull her back to his side, as if they were a pair. It might temporarily ease his ache to hold Jane in his arms again, but it would only serve to further complicate matters.

When the grumble in his stomach told him they'd played the morning away and reminded him he'd never finished his toast, he excused himself from the group to go clean up and check in at work, but not before promising to ask Lucia to start lunch. Alex walked with him back to the house. She'd been away from the twins long enough to get nervous.

Alex held her peace for most of the walk, though Devon could read her well enough to know she had something she wanted to say. She finally succumbed about the time the house came into view.

"Last thing on the topic, I promise." She stopped walking and placed a hand on his arm to still him. "I think you're making a mistake to push Jane away right now. You're hurting her, and you're going to do damage that can't be undone; not easily, anyway."

"I'm trying to not hurt her any worse than I already have."

"You seem so certain that it won't last with her long term that you won't even give it a chance to see if it will. I'm not suggesting you drop down on one knee tonight, Devon. Just get to know her better. See where it goes – be open to the possibility that it will go somewhere. I don't think that's so unreasonable."

Devon raked his fingers through his hair in frustration. "It's just... there is no halfway where she's concerned. From the moment I laid eyes on her, she's had this crazy pull on me. The more I know her, the worse it gets. I don't think I know how to just 'see where it goes.' I just want to whisk her away somewhere and never let her go."

"Then do it. You're rich; that should be one of the bonuses."

Devon opened his mouth to reply then closed it again. He didn't know how to articulate what was really holding him back.

Alex stared into the eyes that so perfectly matched her own before reaching up to kiss his cheek. "She's not the leaving kind. I can't promise you won't get hurt, but you're not avoiding pain right now. You're creating it. I say give it a shot."

With one last hug, she left him to ponder her words. There was a lot of truth to them. He was so intent on mulling over his sister's wisdom that he didn't notice the woman sitting on his patio, watching him walk up the path, until he'd started up the stairs.

"Cassandra." Devon froze. For the briefest of moments, he felt relief to see her standing there because maybe she'd order his phone for him. That relief was instantly replaced by guilt, which was quickly followed by dread. Things were about to get even more complicated.

"Devon."

Having the distinct feeling he was being mentally undressed, he shrugged into his still-damp shirt, greeting her with a polite smile while he buttoned it at least partway up.

"It's good to see you." She seemed nervous.

"You, too. I emailed you just this morning to see how your vacation was going."

"I know. I was already on my way here when I got it. I emailed you back, but I'm guessing you didn't get it."

"Alex murdered my phone." He held it up as if it were proof.

Cass smiled. "Are you enjoying her visit?"

"For the most part."

"I saw the jaguar cubs in the stable. I assume that means you still have house guests?"

"I do."

"Is everything going well there?"

"Are you asking about me and Jane, or are you asking about the jaguar preserve?"

"Both, I guess."

"Actually, I guess the answer is the same for both: It's complicated, but we're trying to get it all sorted out."

"Ah." She was quiet for a moment, a thoughtful look in her eyes. "I'm sorry I added to the list of complications in your life."

Devon went to wave off her apology but she cut him off.

"No, I need to say this."

He nodded slowly, leaning back against the stair railing to wait patiently for her to formulate her words.

"I embarrassed myself, and I caused trouble for you. I'm truly sorry for both. I've put you in an awkward situation, but I'm going to fix it. I've spent a lot of time thinking about what I want to do next. You'll find my resignation on your desk."

"No."

"Yes, you will."

"Okay, but I don't accept it."

"Why? Do you really think we can work together after this?"

"No, and I don't know what the right answer is, but it's not you leaving. You are a part of McAlister Industries. You know it as well as Alex and I do. It's part of who you are, too, and we both know it."

Tears brimmed in Cass's eyes. It was the first time he'd seen a weakness in her defenses. He couldn't help stepping forward to lay a hand on her shoulder.

"I can't live my life waiting for you to feel differently, and as long as you're a constant presence in it, I don't think I'll move on."

"Don't cry, Cassandra. I understand; I do. At least I think I do, but there has to be an answer in between."

Inspiration struck Devon, and he blurted it out before he could change his mind. "What if you oversaw operations back in the States? You'd only have to see me a couple times a year then. Otherwise, it'd be strictly email. It would be a promotion for you, and you'd still be part of the McAlister family. Would that work?"

Cassandra cried even harder, leaving Devon without a response. He knew he'd probably regret it, but he pulled her into his arms in a comforting hug.

"Stop being so nice to me."

"I don't know what to do to fix this, Cass. Are you really that angry at me? I swear I never meant to hurt you. I had no idea how you felt."

"It's not that, Devon. You are the one who should be angry with me. I helped them, damn it. I helped them hurt her. I told myself it was to keep you safe, but I knew how you looked at her. Since she first came here, you haven't been able to keep your eyes off her. Every time we ran into her in the village, you became useless for hours. I knew she was different, that I'd lose you. So I did something terrible." She collapsed against him, her tears inconsolable.

Devon held her helplessly, trying to make sense of her confession.

CHAPTER
SIXTEEN

JANE STOOD, HER FEET ROOTED TO THE GROUND by shock, trying to process the scene before her. Obviously Devon and his beloved Cassandra had kissed and made up now that Devon had taken her advice to "bed Jane and get it over with." Anger bubbled in her veins. She wished she was the type of person who could fly into a rage or, better yet, throw a punch at another human being. She seriously considered learning how to become just such a person.

Daniel and Lani both stood watching her, as if any sudden movements might trigger the explosion Jane was wishing for. Instead of giving in to the fury, she straightened her shoulders, offered her companions a small smile, and excused herself.

She didn't even allow herself tears in the shower, deciding she'd wasted too many on Devon already. Her heart ached to run to him, to figure out why he'd turned a cold shoulder after seeming to actually care about her. Jane firmly reminded herself that his ability to make a woman feel special was why he excelled as a player, which made her even angrier at herself for falling so hard for him. And she had to admit, if only to herself, that she had taken the bait – hook, line, and sinker.

She dressed in jeans and a T-shirt, even that simple act causing her heart to squeeze painfully. As she did her best to tame her hair in a French braid, she chastised herself for reading too much into

Devon's gesture. They'd been nothing more than a stack of clothes, a random act of kindness, not a declaration of feelings.

Snagging her journal from the nightstand where it had lain untouched for days, she slipped down the back stairs. Time in the presence of Aria and Freya would help set her world to right, or at least help her forget it wasn't.

As always, the cats' enthusiastic greeting reminded her she was loved. Every day, they looked less like awkward kittens and more like the predators they would become. Someone had placed an old truck tire in their outdoor enclosure. Jane was happy to see their new toy, but she still wished they could be home, in a more natural setting. She was trying to trust Cody's judgment. It wasn't easy to temper her urge to gather the cubs up and go home, drug lords and terrorists be damned.

After checking to be sure she wasn't sitting in anything gross, Jane curled up in a corner out of sight. Aria went to attack the tire while Freya curled up in a corner of her own. Jane jotted notes in her journal about the growth of the cubs, their adaptability to their new surroundings, and her hopes for reintroducing them to a more naturalized setting. Her observations degraded into a random string of thoughts about Ecuador and life in general, making Jane happy for the ability to edit what she actually shared. She doubted the world in general would care that the power Devon held over her scared the hell out of her or that she was irritated with the universe in general for its arbitrary unfairness.

Jane stopped writing to chew on the end of her pen, wondering what it was she was really trying to accomplish with all the notes anyway. For that matter, what was she truly trying to accomplish here in Ecuador? If she was brutally honest with herself, maybe she'd been hiding behind the jaguars, using them as her shield from humanity. Fat lot of good that had done her.

Aria pounced on Jane's leg, eliciting a wince. Jane reached down to redirect the cub's teeth. "Hey, little girl. That doesn't feel so good. Go get your sister, not me."

Jane pointed Aria in the direction of Freya, who flattened her ears and growled when her sister approached. Jane put her book down and frowned. The sound wasn't at all playful, and that was unlike the adventuresome little cub. She watched the interaction for a moment more before deciding something was definitely wrong.

Cautiously, Jane approached Freya, keeping her voice soft and soothing. The cub let Jane pick her up, her body limp in Jane's arms. It didn't make sense. Freya had seemed okay, if not a little sleepy, when Jane had arrived, and that couldn't have been more than an hour ago. Something was seriously wrong for her to be going downhill so fast.

Cradling the animal to her chest, Jane walked over to the stall door, poking her head out to call for help. Cody answered the call first, having just come back from a ride.

"Jane, I didn't even see you there. Devon's going crazy looking for you back at the house. Daniel told him he was in trouble."

"He's a big boy. He'll survive." Her response was terser than she intended. "Could you find Aldo for me? Something's wrong with Freya."

"Absolutely." He instantly grew serious. "Do you need anything else?"

"Yeah, actually; there's a backpack hanging in the tack room – it has what few supplies I was able to salvage from the preserve. Could you hand me that before you leave?"

Cody did as she asked. Jane shooed Aria into their outdoor pen, closing the bottom half of the door to the stall behind her. After carefully laying Freya in the straw again, Jane sifted through her bag for supplies. A quick examination of the cub left Jane convinced Freya had been poisoned. She couldn't fathom any other explanation for the cub's shallow breathing, rapid heart rate, or extreme lethargy.

Without knowing what had poisoned Freya, Jane had no way of administering an antidote. She didn't even have the basic supplies to administer fluids. Being a biology teacher hadn't prepared her to stabilize a jaguar cub with nothing but her wits and a hodgepodge of supplies. Jane felt completely helpless.

By the time Aldo dropped to his knees beside her, the cub was barely hanging on.

"I don't know what to do." Jane fought the urge to panic, instead rattling off the symptoms she'd been able to ascertain. She was immensely grateful for Aldo's calming presence. He took over, and Jane happily let him. She hurried to follow his every direction, taking a further step back when Maria fell in beside her husband.

With a background in business and not science, Maria may not have had the direct knowledge to save the cub, but she had the ability to read what her husband was thinking. Their effortless communication more than made up for any lack of scientific knowledge.

All Jane could do was watch uselessly as life slipped away from the little black cub she'd tended to since the moment it came into the world. Jane had seen Freya take her first breath. It was with tears in her eyes that she saw her take her last.

Cody tried to pull Jane into a hug, but the kindness in his touch only served to further infuriate her. She was completely and uncontrollably pissed at the world in that moment. It was more than the hopes of the jaguar corridor that lay cold in that horse stall. It was all the love Jane had funneled into those little fur balls that she couldn't give to people. Short of rewinding the clock so Freya could live again, all she really wanted was to find a spot alone in the wilderness so she could rage at the sky.

It was with that thought in mind that Jane stumbled her way out of the stable. Once she was free of the building, she ran. She didn't know where she was headed, nor did she care. She simply ran.

When her legs could carry her no farther and her lungs refused another moment's torture, she sank to the ground, pounding her fist into the dirt as she shouted. She didn't know where the words came from that tumbled out of her mouth; they just came.

She heard the horse before she ever saw Cody emerge from the trees. He didn't say anything at first. He didn't even get down off the black beast. He sat stoically, giving her space and time to grieve. When she had no more words to shout and no more energy to spend, she sat regarding him silently.

He cracked a hint of that easy grin of his. "I thought you might need a ride back, darlin'."

Jane considered reminding him she didn't ride. She was actually terrified of horses, having been thrown from one as a child. But it was a long walk back, and Cody looked like he'd been born in a saddle. Surely she'd be safe with him.

She stood, feeling much older than she was, and wiped off her jeans. After a vain attempt to straighten her appearance, she accepted Cody's hand up. He swung her onto the saddle behind him with uncanny ease. The horse didn't even flinch at the motion, somewhat calming Jane's apprehension at being so high off the ground.

Jane wrapped her arms around his waist and laid her head against his back. Cody patted her hand reassuringly before gathering his reins and quietly urging the horse forward. They didn't go straight back. Jane wasn't fully aware of the direction she'd headed during her earlier flight, but she was familiar enough with her surroundings to know they were taking a meandering route. She appreciated his giving her time to collect herself.

The easy rhythm of the horse's footfalls, the gentle sway of Cody's hips as he moved with the animal, there was something very soothing in it all. Ever so slowly, the pain ebbed away, making room for rational thought again. He didn't talk, and he didn't try to make her feel better. His presence and his strength were enough.

When he eased her back to the ground at the bottom of the patio stairs, she looked up at him with a small smile. "Devon must have really messed with my head."

"Why do you say that?"

"It's the only explanation for why I'm not tripping over myself to get to you. I don't know who you were, or what you did to her, but one day the woman you love will see the man you've become, and she won't be able to help loving him. You'll see. It'll be okay."

Cody dipped his head in acknowledgement before winking at her and moving the horse along. Jane could almost picture him with a six shooter on his side. Men like Cody Kingsley gave cowboys a good name.

Jane had no desire to see anybody, though she knew it couldn't be avoided. When she walked through the door, Devon started toward her but was stilled by his sister, who put a restraining hand on his arm. The look on Alex's face reached out to Jane as effectively as a hug.

Cassandra sat quietly on the couch with her hands folded neatly in her lap. She stared at the ground as if not wanting to draw attention to herself. Daniel sat on the arm of a chair in between the two women; his posture led Jane to believe he was prepared to intercede should they leap at each other. The children were conspicuously absent.

"Has anyone heard, is Aria okay?" Jane asked.

"She's fine. It doesn't appear that she ingested whatever Freya got into," Alex reassured her.

"Did anyone figure out what it was?"

Daniel shook his head. "We've searched every inch of their enclosure. Someone had to have directly poisoned her."

Jane was painfully aware that Devon's eyes never left her. She didn't know what to make of the expression on his face, nor was she certain she cared at the moment. She stiffened her spine, lest she appear weak.

"Wouldn't someone have to know the pass code to get on the compound? I mean, don't workers come and go at certain times? Wouldn't it have triggered the alarm if someone breached the fence?" Jane frowned, trying to wrap her mind around what was going on. "Did someone here do it? Why? That makes no sense."

"We don't really know what happened or who did it." Devon stepped free of his sister's grasp, stopping short of Jane. He lifted his hands as if to put them on her shoulders before dropping them back to his sides again. "I can't imagine it was anyone here. I trust them."

"And I trusted you. Sometimes trust doesn't work out so well for us." Jane's eyes met his. She sincerely hoped hers sparked with half as much anger as she felt.

"I'm not sure what you think you saw, but I promise you it's a misunderstanding. We should probably talk alone once we're sure we aren't about to be attacked."

"There really isn't anything to say." Jane looked away, mentally cursing herself for nearly getting caught in his gaze so easily. "You just did what you do best and I fell for it. It's an age-old story. No sense rehashing it now when there are more important things going on."

Devon sucked in his breath as if holding back what he really wanted to say. "Damn it, Jane," he growled.

"They have the pass code," Cassandra interrupted, causing a hush to fall over the room.

Devon turned slowly to face Cass, his voice low and steady as he spoke. "How do you know that? What did you mean earlier, when you said you helped them hurt her?"

All eyes locked on the small blonde trying to look even smaller on the couch. Cass glanced at Jane and then sought Devon's eyes.

Jane couldn't understand what passed between them or begin to fathom what she had to do with it.

When at last Cass began to speak, it was barely above a whisper. "Javier cornered me in the market one day. He told me that he needed to put in a new road, and if I didn't want them to bulldoze a path through the plantation, then I had to help them clear out the preserve."

Jane felt like she'd been sucker punched in the gut. She didn't move or speak; she didn't trust herself to.

"You gave them the pass code to the compound alarm system?" Devon clarified.

"I was going to ask security to change it, but then we got into that fight and I left."

"Forget putting the entire plantation at risk – our livelihoods at risk; you handed them Jane and the Guerreros? How could you do that?" Devon looked so wounded that for one crazy second, Jane wanted to reach out and comfort him.

"He threatened to wipe out everything we'd worked so hard for. I took a calculated risk." Cass straightened, her gaze hardening.

"Didn't you even care what would happen to Jane?"

"No, not really," Cass admitted. Jane recoiled; she'd never been so hated before. "Nobody wants those cats she's trying to reintroduce. This plantation fuels an entire village. Who does the preserve help besides a bunch of scientists?"

"Those cats are an integral part of a perfectly balanced ecosystem." Alex moved to stand by Jane, wrapping an arm around her for support. "But even if you didn't care about them, it wasn't for you to put their lives at risk."

The room seemed to swirl around Jane. It had been one thing to have her home so callously ripped away by a drug lord, a known evil. But to know that heinous act was abetted by a jealous woman over a man who didn't love either of them was more than Jane could stomach. She'd never done anything to this person, but she was about to.

Breaking free of Alex's comforting hug, Jane launched herself at Cass. Devon moved faster, wrapping his arms around Jane's waist and lifting her off her feet to spin her away from Cassandra. That didn't stop Jane from kicking and squirming in an attempt to break free and launch a new assault.

"Ow!. Damn it, Jane. Stop that. This isn't like you." Devon set her on the ground but didn't loosen his grip.

"How do you know what is and isn't like me?" Jane whirled to face him despite their close proximity. "You don't want to know me because then you might feel something resembling an emotion. Stay out of this."

"I'm not going to just step back and let you beat the hell out of my assistant."

"That might not be a bad idea," Daniel interjected.

"You're not helping." Devon cast a quick glare Daniel's way before looking back to Jane. He caught her eyes with his and lowered his voice. "Remember Micah 6:8, Jane."

She narrowed her eyes and growled back. "You don't even know what it means."

"I do too. I Googled it."

Jane took a deep breath and blinked back tears. "Where was *her* mercy? Where's the justice for Freya, for Deifilia? Where's my justice? I'm tired of living by a stupid verse!"

"You don't mean that." Devon shook his head, pulling her into his arms. She stiffened, not wanting to melt into him. "Love, we both know you don't mean it. Please say you don't. You can't control what other people do, only how you react to it. Up until this moment, you've been the ray of sunshine in my dark world. You're what gives me hope that it's not all pointless. Don't take that hope away."

Jane felt her resolve slipping. It would be so easy to rest her head against him and let the tears flow.

"Why do you even care?" Her stance softened; she felt the fight wick away from her body.

"I care because I care about you. Very much." He kissed the top of her head.

She didn't believe him, not really, but it was still good to stop fighting his embrace. It felt right to be in his arms, like maybe the big, bad world wouldn't win after all. She rested her head on his chest and stared at nothing in particular. She might have decided not to kill Cassandra with her bare hands, but she wasn't going to cry in front of her, either.

"I'm sorry," Cassandra spoke, the malice gone from her voice. "I can't begin to tell you how sorry I am."

"Honestly? I don't really care how sorry you are at this particular moment." Jane was brutally honest. "Deifilia and Freya are dead. Words can't undo that, and they certainly didn't deserve it."

Silence hung in the air between them. After an awkward moment, Alex leaned over to Daniel and whispered, "What's Micah 6:8?"

"It's a Bible verse," Daniel replied, not bothering to whisper. "'He has shown you, O man, what is good; and what does the Lord require of you but to do justly, to love mercy, and to walk humbly with your God?'"

"How did you know that?" Alex wondered.

"Vacation Bible School. That one kind of stuck with me." Daniel shrugged.

Jane couldn't help a small smile at that. She gently pushed herself away from Devon, needing to break the contact between them before she got too used to it again. "I might not be ready to show mercy, but I promise I'll control myself now."

Devon loosened his grip but didn't completely break contact. His hand rested lightly on her elbow.

"I don't understand," Alex mused aloud. "Why did he need to go through Devon's to get to Jane? Why kill the cats?"

"I don't know." Daniel shook his head. "It doesn't make any sense to me, either."

"He's got to be setting me up for something," Devon agreed. "And if he's had my pass code for weeks, who knows how deeply he's infiltrated our security system?"

"If that's the case, I'm not waiting around for him to kill the last cub just to get to you," Jane decided. "I'm sorry – I don't mean to sound callous – but I'm going to make sure Aria is safe. If we can't get back our piece of the corridor, at least she can go into a breeding plan somewhere else along the basin."

"I don't think it's safe for you to leave," Devon protested.

"And I appreciate both your concern and your hospitality, but this is something I need to decide with Maria and Aldo." Her words were calm but firm.

She didn't look back. She couldn't, not without running the risk of falling under his spell again. Aria was now the best and only hope of saving the jaguar population in her stretch of the Amazon Basin. She'd failed Deifilia and Freya. She wasn't going to fail Aria, no matter what it took.

CHAPTER
SEVENTEEN

DEVON HAD STARED AT THE CLOSED DOOR long after Jane walked out, willing her to come back through it. When she didn't, he'd grudgingly dealt with the room full of people he wished he could ignore. He hadn't the first clue what to do with Cassandra after her admission. Until he figured it out, she was put on leave and relieved of her duties. He couldn't fathom trusting her again, but he also didn't have the heart to turn her out after so many years of faithful service. It was a conundrum he'd have to figure out when his life and livelihood weren't on the line.

It didn't seem right to Devon that the world continued to turn as if Jane had never crossed his path. He knew everyone was biding time, giving Cody a chance to put his men into play, but it felt an awful lot like the rest of the universe simply forgot Jane existed. He didn't know how to do that.

Unable to bear the reminder of the cubs, Devon cleaned out their stall. Memories swirled around him as he shoveled the straw into a wheelbarrow, making the chore all the harder. It was almost as if by being there, he could hear her laughter or feel her head resting on his shoulder. Just as he was finishing the last corner, he found Jane's journal.

Holding the book in his hands made the longing for her that much stronger. Deciding to return it to her via Maria or Aldo, he tucked the journal into his pocket and finished the task he'd set out to do. There was a finality to seeing the empty stall that bothered him almost as much as staring at the door after it had closed behind Jane.

The weight of the book in his pocket was the only thing Devon could think about the rest of the day. By that evening, it had become an obsession. After tossing the book on his nightstand, he went to shower. Maybe enough cold water would roust her from his mind.

He emerged from his shower frigid but in no better mental shape than he was upon entering. When he climbed into bed, he tried to sleep but found himself staring at the book instead. He couldn't stand it anymore. Muttering to himself, he flipped on the light and sat up, swiping the book off the nightstand and flipping through the pages. Her distinctive feminine script leapt out at him and he could almost hear the sound of her voice as he read. It felt like she was there with him again.

He was instantly pulled in by her words, captivated by seeing Ecuador and his home through her eyes. Somewhere in the back of his mind, guilt reared its ugly head. He could have sat up all night, soaking in her every thought, but he would rather hear them from her lips. Gently, he closed the book and placed it in his drawer, lest he be tempted to open it again. It was a long time before sleep claimed him that night.

After two more days of moping and making stupid mistakes at work because his mind was elsewhere, he tried going for a horseback ride with Cody to clear his head. Walking past the now empty stall that had once housed the cubs brought it all crashing back, though. It seemed cleaning the straw out had done nothing to erase the memories. He forced himself to see the ride through anyway. He knew he was in danger of becoming a hermit otherwise.

Cody broke the silence on their way home. "Has your security team found any breaches?"

"Nope." Devon shook his head. "All the pass codes have been reset, and they've pored over the logs. Other than one unauthorized gate use the day Freya was killed, Barrera hasn't made a move."

"Why would a guy who collects cats use his ace in the hole to kill a panther cub that posed no threat to him whatsoever?" Cody mused.

"I don't get it, either. Or Deifilia's collar – I get that they had the pass code, that's how they got it here, but why? All that accomplished was bringing me into the mix. I wouldn't have known anything about what was going on if Jane hadn't triggered that alarm. And by her own admission, my getting involved with Jane was exactly what Cassandra was trying to avoid."

"I feel like we need another piece or two of the puzzle to start putting it all into place."

"I can't help but think he isn't going after me because my name is too visible. If Alex or I went missing, it would still make news back in the States," Devon theorized.

"Hezbollah has been able to infiltrate countries all over the globe by keeping the Western world largely ignorant of just how many pies they have their finger in." Cody thought for a moment. "So you're probably right. You and Alex are most likely safe enough even without me here."

"The question is this: If Javier believed Jane was taking the cubs and going home, what was he trying to accomplish by killing Freya?" Devon wondered aloud.

"Who says he believed her story?"

"Could be. But if he did...."

"Then he could have been trying to flush Jane out from under your protection," Cody finished Devon's sentence.

It sickened Devon to think that his actions had placed Jane in danger – that she was left to face Barrera alone because he'd failed.

"Wipe that defeated look off your face, Devon. We're still in the game. It's just time to rethink our strategy." Cody's tone was sympathetic. "I'll take off first thing in the morning so I can meet with my contact sooner. We'll see if we can't get someone down here by the end of the week. In the meantime, have Alex warn Jane that Barrera might come after her and that other cub. They're tucked away safe and sound for the moment, but just in case she had any bright ideas about sticking her head out, she shouldn't."

"Wait...." Realization struck Devon. "Alex knows where Jane is?"

"She visits her every day. Haven't you noticed her absent for long chunks of the day?"

"I thought she was avoiding me because she was mad." Devon furrowed his brow. "Why does Alex get to know where she is and I don't?"

Cody shrugged. "I guess she figures if you know, Cassandra might find out. I can't blame her for not trusting Cass just yet."

"But she can trust me." Devon was trying not to pout.

"That's a discussion for the two of you. I'm staying out if it." Cody urged his mount to pick up the pace, making Devon wonder if he was running away from the conversation. He let it go, not bothering to keep up with his friend. Devon needed time to think, and the fresh air was good for him.

Without paying much attention to where he was going, he found himself on the path to the little cabin where he'd taken Jane that day not so long ago. It felt like a lifetime since he'd stood debating whether or not he should peel her wet clothes off after she'd collapsed. Thinking about it now, pain squeezed his heart.

Hope quickly replaced the pain when he realized the cabin was occupied. It was the perfect place to hide from Barrera. He urged his horse to pick up the pace, a smile breaking as he neared the little building. He'd talk to her, just the two of them, and they'd set this thing right between them.

Only the teenage boy who emerged from the cabin was decidedly not Jane. The dark-headed youth took one look at Devon and began to run. Devon easily caught up to the boy, throwing himself off the horse to tackle him before he could dive into the undergrowth. The two men tussled for a few moments before Devon had his opponent subdued.

"*No haga daño a mi, por favor.*" The teenager's voice cracked.

"I'm not going to hurt you," Devon assured him. "Do you understand English?"

The boy nodded.

"Good. If I let you up, will you stay put?"

The boy nodded again.

"I mean it. If I have to chase you, I'm going to be pissed."

"I won't run," he promised.

Devon responded by easing his grip. The kid bolted. Devon swore under his breath and took off after him. After the second tackle and tussle, once Devon again had his opponent subdued, he wasn't willing to take any more chances. This time, he pulled the small revolver from his boot. Once the teenager saw it, he began apologizing profusely in Spanish.

"Relax, kid. I'm not going to shoot you," Devon promised before cracking him over the head with the butt of the gun. Once he was sure the teenager was out, he added, "But I am too tired to chase you again."

He took off his belt to secure the young man's arms before going in search of some rope in the house. When he found some, he came back to re-secure his prisoner. He whistled for the horse twice before giving up and tossing the kid over his shoulder like a sack of potatoes. He groaned under the weight but resolutely trudged back toward the house.

Thankfully he didn't have far to go before Cody found them. "I got worried when your horse came back without you."

"Disloyal beast," Devon muttered, glad the gelding had at least gone back to the stables. He dropped the teenager on the ground beside him and rubbed his shoulders.

"So, uh, who's this?" Cody asked when no explanation seemed forthcoming.

"He was living in the cabin. When he wouldn't quit running away, I decided it might be easier to bring him in asleep. Now I question that logic. The kid's heavier than he looks."

Cody smiled and swung off his own horse. "We can toss him up here."

After a bit of maneuvering, they had the boy tossed over the horse and were on their way. They spent the rest of the walk discussing who he could possibly be.

"One thing I keep thinking," Devon uttered, "is that he might be the missing puzzle piece we were looking for."

"Or some random kid you conked over the head," Cody countered, a grin tugging at the corner of his mouth.

"A trespassing kid," Devon amended.

"Remind me never to bring my kids to visit you," Cody joked.

"But if they're here visiting, they aren't trespassing. And do you really think you'll settle down and have kids someday? I thought you'd made bachelorhood an art form."

"Said the pot to the kettle. And that wasn't very nice of you."

"You're right. I'm being an ass. Sorry." Rather than further alienate his friend, Devon sank into a moody silence.

By the time they emerged from the jungle, there was a search party gathering at the house. Apparently word had spread quickly around the compound that Devon's horse had come back alone. Alex launched herself at him before he even came to a stop.

"You scared me," she admonished.

"Sorry. It's kind of a long story."

"Does the story explain why you've got a guy hog-tied over the back of Cody's horse?" Daniel asked.

"It does," Devon answered. "Do you want to help me get him to the couch?"

"By all means."

"I'm glad you didn't get eaten by a jaguar or anything, Uncle Devon." Lani gave him a half-hug on her way by.

"Thanks. Me too." Devon didn't bother telling her the odds of there being an adult jaguar on his property were pretty slim.

One of the twins began crying while they were still struggling to get the boy into the house. Alex hurried off to respond, leaving them with the order to wait until she got back to say anything important.

Apparently the boy didn't realize Alex's directive was intended for him, too, because the second she was out of the room, he began to rouse.

"Sorry I hit you." Devon knelt beside the boy to offer him a drink of water. "If you'd stop fighting me and answer a few questions, I'm sure we can get this all straightened out in no time."

"And then you'll untie me?"

"I'll untie you now if you'll stay put," Devon offered. "Only this time you have to really do it, because you're surrounded and I'm out of patience."

"I will. I promise." The boy nodded.

"Good." Devon began working at the knots binding the boy. "Now how about you tell me your name? I'm Devon."

"The rose grower." The boy noticeably relaxed. "I'm Eduardo."

"Yes, I'm the rose grower. So tell me, Eduardo, why were you at the cabin?"

Eduardo didn't answer at first. His gaze shifted from Devon to Daniel to Cody.

"It's okay. They're friends of mine."

After another moment's hesitation, the boy began to spill everything he knew, from the moment he'd first laid eyes on Jane to the moment he cracked her over the head in a desperate attempt to keep her safe.

"I thought you were going to wait for me," Alex protested upon re-entering the room.

Devon cast a glance her way, offering his sister a brief smile before turning back to Eduardo. "The jaguar Deifilia, she was wearing a collar...."

"I know," Eduardo jumped in excitedly. "I took it."

"You took the collar? Did you kill Deifilia, too?"

Eduardo looked horrified. "No, I wouldn't dare! The cat was already dead when I found her. But I knew the blonde would look for that collar. So I broke into your compound and threw it in a tree. I wanted her to find you."

"Why did you want her to find me?" Devon struggled to keep up.

"Because everyone knows you, that you're a good man. I wanted you to protect her."

Devon sat back, considering Eduardo's words. "What happened after you threw the collar in the tree?"

"I hid. I didn't know what else to do. I thought I would be safe here until I figured it out."

Though he couldn't say why, Devon believed the young man. "Just one more question: Why did you cross Barrera? Why help Jane at all?"

"Because it was the right thing to do," Eduardo answered without hesitation.

Devon found it hard to believe that this teenager had risked his life to save three strangers simply because it was the right thing to do, but then again, maybe that was more a reflection on himself than this boy. Either way, it seemed to him that Eduardo had earned a rest and a hot meal.

After arranging for both, and for someone to keep an eye on Eduardo just in case, Devon decided it was time to try appealing to his sister's better nature. He'd persuade her to take him to Jane. Maybe then they could straighten out some of the many miscommunications they'd had recently.

Only his sister seemed to be avoiding him. The day after Eduardo arrived, Cody left. Devon still wasn't sure what to do with Eduardo, but he wasn't willing to turn the young man out; to do so would be a death sentence. If Javier saw his former employee on Devon's plantation, that wouldn't bode well for anybody. Still, Devon felt he owed the boy Jane's life. The best answer he could find was to give the young man a job in one of the greenhouses, where he'd be less likely to be seen. At night, the boy stayed as a guest in Devon's home. It didn't take long at all for Devon to get used to having him around.

Devon tried for days to get Alex alone, to no avail. She was either surrounded by her family or nowhere to be seen. On the third day, she seemed to have disappeared altogether. Devon finally relinquished his pride to ask Daniel her whereabouts. Daniel's answer was vague enough to tell Devon exactly where Alex was.

"Does everyone know where Jane is except me?" Devon surmised, scowling.

"I don't know the specifics," Daniel hedged.

"Like hell you don't," Devon rebutted. "There's no way you'd let Alex get that far away from you without knowing where she was headed, especially not when you're already worried about her safety."

"True," Daniel admitted. "But I'm also smart enough not to cross my lovely wife. If she wants to keep Jane's location concealed from you, then you're going to have to talk to her about that."

"You and Cody are both very adept at hot potato. Do you know that?"

"It's an acquired skill. It comes in handy for both political careers and marriages."

"Well, when my sister reappears, could you please tell her I'm looking for her? I mean, if that isn't taking too much of a stand and all."

Daniel only smiled at the barb. "You mock now. You'll be there soon enough."

"How can I be anywhere other than here, if nobody will tell me where Jane is so I can have a conversation with her? Everyone is after me to tell her how I feel, but I can't do that if you've hidden her from me!" Devon finally exploded.

Daniel's grin only deepened. "And what exactly would you tell her, if you could find her?"

The wind was knocked out of Devon's sails with that question. Anger evaporated as he thought for a moment. "I'd tell her that I love her, and I don't ever want to see her walk out that door again, not without knowing she intends to come back."

"That should do the trick. I guess it wouldn't hurt to tell you that Alex plans on taking Jane dancing tonight. She thinks Jane needs a break, and dancing is Alex's solution to everything."

"I don't think that's such a good idea." Devon frowned. "I'm not sure it was me Javier was after when he used those pass codes."

"You think he was after Jane?"

"That's what I'm afraid of, yes."

Daniel seemed to be mulling over the options in his mind before speaking. "Either way, your best chance at getting close to her without leading Javier straight to her is at the cabana tonight. I've already sent a small security detail to sweep the place. They'll stick around as long as Alex is there. That should dissuade Javier from doing anything stupid."

Devon nodded, knowing he wasn't going to get anything else out of Daniel. Maybe they were right. Maybe it was best he didn't know where Jane was keeping the cub; the temptation to make a beeline straight there would be too great. As it was now, he found himself eagerly watching the clock, counting down the minutes until he could head to the village bar without running the risk of scaring her away.

Nighttime had never seemed so far away.

CHAPTER
EIGHTEEN

JANE SMILED AS SHE WATCHED Alex walk down the little dirt path leading to the hut Jane had called home for the past week. Since leaving Devon's, she'd been staying with one of the families who worked at the plantation. She'd left the clothes from Devon at his house, so they'd even provided her with clothing in the traditional style of their little village. The bright blue skirt and white blouse were more comfortable than she would have supposed.

Jane did her best to help the family in return for their kindness. While they worked at the factory, Jane stayed behind to care for Aria and tackle what chores she knew how to do. She knew she couldn't hide in this little hut forever, but it seemed to be her best option for now.

Every day Alex came to visit with food for Aria and news to reassure Jane they'd be reclaiming her preserve soon. It didn't sit well with Jane to wait on the sidelines for someone else to save her. Still, taking down a terrorist-backed drug ring was decidedly new territory for her. If Cody Kingsley had some ninjas up his sleeve that would take care of it, more power to him.

On this particular day, Alex was coming with more than food and news: She came insisting that Jane go with her to the village's lone little bar, the place of Jane and Devon's first real conversation. No matter how many times Jane protested, Alex persisted, eventually wearing Jane down.

Once she found herself sitting in the middle of a crowded room with music pulsing all around her, she began to wish she'd shown better resolve. As it was, she sipped her sangria, missed Devon terribly, and tried not to waste what little time she had left with Alex. Jane hadn't realized how badly she'd needed a friend until she found one. Now, she dreaded Alex's departure.

"Don't look now, but we have company." Alex leaned toward Jane, nodding in the direction of the newcomer.

"Devon?" Jane's heart skipped.

"No, but the way your face brightened just then was cute." Alex grinned. "Unfortunately it's your other neighbor who strolled in."

"Darn." Jane wrinkled her nose. "He gives me the creeps."

"Understandable."

"Remind me why I'm still playing nice with this guy."

"Element of surprise," Alex whispered.

"Right." Jane took a deep breath. She could do this. She considered ordering another sangria, but Alex dragged her onto the dance floor before she could act on it. While the crowd still made her feel slightly claustrophobic, Jane had to admit it was fun to be silly with Alex on the dance floor.

The pulsating music gave way to the gentler strains of a slow song. Jane went to follow Alex back to their table but was intercepted by Javier.

"Could I persuade you to dance with me?" He bowed slightly.

Jane wracked her brain for an excuse not to. She opened her mouth to answer, still not quite sure what her answer would be, when a hand took her elbow even as another pressed the small of her back. Devon's voice rumbled low behind her. "I'm sorry, Javier. I'm afraid she's already promised this dance to me."

Without waiting for a response from Javier or even Jane, Devon pulled her back onto the dance floor and into his arms.

"I can't decide if I'm irritated or relieved," Jane admitted, thoroughly unsettled by how incredible it felt to be back in his arms.

"You're relieved," he decided for her. "Or you will be when you find out that I think Javier didn't kill Freya to get to me but you."

Jane took a moment to hide the shock and fury, lest her body language telegraph it across the room. "Why? What on earth do I have to offer him?"

Devon's voice grew gentle. "Have you seen yourself? You're a goddess. Javier collects more than cats."

"Oh." Nausea gripped Jane's stomach at the thought of being part of Javier's collection. Still, she struggled to believe everything Devon said. "I'm hardly a goddess, and flattery won't get me back in your bed, Devon."

"You really have such a dim view of me?"

She knew she'd hurt him; she could hear it in his voice, see it in his wounded eyes. She hadn't meant to be callous. Without thinking, she reached up to run her fingertips down the side of his face. "No, I don't think ill of you. I'm sorry. We're just very different people. That's all."

"The differences are what make it fun." He grinned briefly before growing serious again. "I don't have long before this song is over and you slip out of my grasp again, so I have to say what I came to."

"Is everything okay?" Jane was worried about him.

"Everything's fine," he promised. "I just think we got our wires crossed somewhere. I think some of my actions might have been misinterpreted...."

"You don't have to explain yourself to me. You're a big boy. It's none of my business," Jane interrupted.

"Stop saying that." Anger flashed across Devon's face before he reined it in. "It is your business. I thought we were in a relationship, or at least the beginnings of one, and that makes it your business."

"We were?" Jane's heart hammered in her ears as she tried to sort out what he was saying.

"You assumed because of my reputation that I didn't want a relationship. I never said that."

"But Cass said...."

"Cass is a woman with a broken heart who'd mistakenly thought she had a claim to me. Hell hath no fury and all that."

"But you pulled away. I could feel it. You started backpedaling the instant you got what you wanted."

"I was scared," he admitted, his voice oozing exasperation. "Thank you very much for making me say that one out loud. I was terrified I'd care too much and then you'd leave, only that happened anyway."

The music ended but neither made a move to release the other. They stood still in the middle of the dance floor as it filled again with bodies pulsating to the music. Jane didn't know what to say, what to believe.

"Janey, I love you. I don't care how crazy that sounds." He took her face in his hands, peering deep into her eyes before continuing. "Just so we're on the same page, from this point on I am dedicating myself to two things: getting us out of this alive and winning your love."

Jane struggled to breathe. She wanted desperately to grab hold of what he was offering with both hands and never look back. "I guess it's my turn to admit to being scared. I don't know that I can love you without losing me."

Incredible sadness descended across his features. His hands fell from her face to rest lightly on her shoulders. She felt like the world's biggest jerk. She would have given just about anything to make that look of sorrow go away, but then that was the problem. She'd thought she was in love with Sam. She'd given up her dreams of being a field biologist to teach science in the same sleepy Arkansas town she'd dreamt of escaping – only for him to leave her the instant she was no longer a perfect fit for his perfect plan.

Jane leaned up and kissed Devon. Maybe it was her goodbye. More likely it was so she could feel his lips on hers one more time. Even she couldn't say what she was hoping to accomplish with that kiss. Whatever it was, all she really accomplished was making herself cry in public.

Devon brushed the tears from her cheeks. "Don't cry, love. It'll be okay."

"I wish I could give you what you want. I'm just not ready."

"Then I'll wait until you are." He brushed her lips with a gentle kiss.

"And if that day never comes?"

"Then someday the village kids will make up stories about crazy old Mr. McAlister. They'll all have their own theory as to why I became a mad old hermit. But no pressure or anything."

Jane laughed. "You are such a brat."

"Please come home, though. I'd feel so much safer with you at the plantation. I'll give you as much time and space as you need."

Knowing Javier was after her in particular scared her more than she was willing to admit. Devon was right; she'd be safer in his home than anywhere else. Especially now that the security codes had been updated and they knew what kind of threat they were watching for. She nodded.

He beamed at her response. "Wonderful. I can send a security team to pick up Aria tonight if you'd like."

Jane shook her head at that one. "No, if I'm what Javier is after, then I'd be putting Aria in danger to bring her back. I think it would be safer to send her to stay with Maria and Aldo at her sister's house."

"Whatever you want," Devon quickly agreed. "I'll arrange for it right away."

"Thank you." Jane allowed Devon to wind his fingers around hers and lead her off the dance floor. A drunken tourist stumbled into them at the edge of the crowd.

Devon reached out to set the silver-haired man straight. "Are you okay?"

"Watch where you're walking, lover boy," he sneered, thumping Devon on the chest.

Jane's eyebrows shot up. She opened her mouth to retort when Devon jumped in, tugging her closer to his side as he replied. "Sure. No harm done, though, right?"

The man didn't answer, shoving away from Devon to stumble toward a pretty young brunette who reached out to steady him.

Jane watched in disgust as the pair stumbled out of the bar, arm in arm. "I don't even know what to say to that."

Devon leaned down to whisper in Jane's ear. "Don't react when I tell you this, but he planted something on me during the altercation. I'm sure of it."

She smiled as if he'd whispered sweet nothings then reached up to kiss his cheek. "Should we go?"

"Yeah. Let's grab Alex and head out."

Despite Devon's promise to give her space, he didn't let go of her hand until they were safely in the Jeep. When he did, her fingers felt bereft. They itched to reach forward and touch him again. Alex was thrilled to hear Jane would be coming back to Devon's. It meant she could spend her last day in Ecuador with both of them.

"I want to know what that guy planted on you." Jane waited until they were alone on the road to Devon's before bringing it up. Alex's security detail was in the cars in front of and behind them.

"Here." Devon reached into his shirt pocket to fish out a piece of paper, which he handed to Alex in the seat beside him.

She turned on the interior light and opened the note, reading aloud. "Friends of the lion. Turn perimeter fences off from 11:04 to 11:06 p.m. UTC-6."

"Who's the lion?" Jane didn't understand.

"Cody, I think," Devon answered. "He said his operatives would identify themselves as friends of the lion, anyway."

"So the stumbling drunk was the savior Cody promised?" Jane frowned. "That's fantastic news."

"What are you going to do?" Alex handed the note back.

Devon shrugged and sighed. "Turn off the fences for two minutes tonight, I guess."

They were all on pins and needles waiting for 11:04 to arrive. That didn't stop Jane from taking a hot shower and changing into lounge pants and a T-shirt. She told herself over and over that the man had most likely been playing the part of a fool in order to pass the note to Devon. Until he confirmed as much, though, she couldn't help being more scared than ever.

The stark thought settled over her that if Cody's help wasn't as competent as he'd led them to believe, she would lose her preserve forever. For that matter, she'd be lucky to escape Ecuador with both her life and freedom. The thought of leaving Ecuador was almost her undoing. She hadn't realized before that moment just how much the country had come to mean to her, how endearing its people, how beautiful its land. She realized with a start it was more than a jaguar preserve she was fighting for; it was her home.

At the precise moment, Devon shut off the fence from the computer in his office. Jane sat curled in the big leather wingback chair in the corner. Alex and Daniel sat side by side on the matching sofa, their posture alert. Each had placed a hand in between them, their fingers touching lightly. Jane knew Daniel would want to be ready for battle, but that didn't stop him from seeking some form of contact with Alex.

Jane loved that about the couple. They were each strong individuals. Together, they seemed invincible. To Jane, they were the one pair in a million. It took one hell of a man to not fear a woman's strength – and a woman with true strength not to yield it in the name of love. Jane knew that's what she was afraid of. It wasn't any action on Devon's part; that had just been her excuse. She had no doubt he was man enough to uphold his end of the deal. It was her own lack of strength that really scared her.

Exactly two minutes after lowering the plantation's defenses, Devon had them back up and running. Everyone in the room braced for the sound of an alarm. The silence was unsettling. Jane wondered if it meant the man had cleared the fence in time or if he was even there.

"What now?" Jane finally voiced what she imagined everyone was thinking.

"Do we go to the receiving room?" Alex suggested.

"I'm not sure someone who scaled the fence to avoid being seen is going to ring the doorbell," Devon reasoned. "My vote is that I pour us all a drink and we wait right here. If he does ring the doorbell, the staff will let him in. If not, Daniel's posted security at all of the entry points."

"Are you trying to get us all as tipsy as the ninja?" Jane teased.

"I'm hardly a ninja," a new male voice countered from the window. "And I apologize for my appearance earlier. It was a necessary diversion."

"You missed a spot." Alex looked at Daniel and nodded towards the window.

Devon rose, placing himself between the man and the others in the room as the stranger stepped into the light and extended a hand. "It's good to officially meet you, Devon. I'm Atlas."

"Atlas?" Jane repeated curiously, rising to stand beside Devon.

"In my line of work, code names are preferable. It's been so long since I've gone by my given name, I'm afraid I wouldn't answer even if you called it," he explained.

"Fair enough." She extended a hand in greeting. "I'm Jane Russell."

"From the jaguar preserve." Recognition dawned in his eyes. "It's good to meet you."

"Thank you for coming."

"Yes, thank you," Devon added before turning to the pair on the couch. "This is my sister, Alex, and her husband, Daniel. They'll be leaving day after tomorrow. I'd prefer we not do anything to piss Barrera off until after they leave, if possible."

"If we do our job right, he won't know where to direct his ire," Atlas assured them. "But nonetheless, I see no harm in waiting a day to make a move. It will give us time to ascertain the layout of the compound and coordinate with other interested parties."

"Us?" Devon prompted.

"Forgive me." Atlas held his hand out to the window to assist the pretty brunette from the bar, though it was obvious she didn't need his help. "Please allow me to introduce my associate, Robin."

"Is that a code name or an actual name?" Jane wondered, shaking the woman's hand. At five-foot-two with a lithe build, she didn't exactly look fierce. Jane almost wondered if hummingbird might not have been more apropos.

The young woman smiled endearingly. Whatever Robin brought to the table, Jane appreciated her willingness to trek to the jungles of Ecuador to help Jane reclaim her home.

"Please come in and sit down. I was just getting ready to pour everyone a drink. Can I get you one?"

"I'd better not. I'm trying to re-establish Ms. Russell's faith in me." Atlas winked at Jane.

She could feel her cheeks heat with embarrassment. "I'll take one, Devon."

Atlas chuckled. "Then I guess I'll take one after all."

Robin rolled her eyes and shook her head. "Don't let him get to you. He's an acquired taste, but he is very good at what he does."

"And he's not deaf," Atlas added, his playful expression setting Jane's mind at ease.

"What's the plan?" Daniel brought the conversation back.

"Kill Barrera. Don't get caught," Atlas answered.

"While your plan is devastatingly brilliant in its simplicity, would you mind connecting the dots for us a bit?" Devon handed Robin and Atlas both a glass before returning to pour Jane's.

"Fair enough," Atlas conceded. "The only reason Barrera even started looking for a new route is because of us. Well, indirectly us.

We made the Drug Enforcement Agency look bad when we rounded up a drug ring they'd taken bribes from, so they started putting the squeeze on Barrera to redeem themselves in the eyes of the administration. We'll simply convince Barrera's backers that this corridor is no longer viable at all."

"How?" Maybe it was morbid curiosity that prompted her to ask because Jane wasn't sure she wanted to understand everything that went on behind the scenes.

"The DEA is planning to intercept a shipment heading across your preserve this week. While Javier is busy dealing with that, we'll strike his compound. If I can take out the factory, if we can cost them enough money and make it look like it was an official U.S. action, they'll look elsewhere. They're not quite ready to take on the big dogs just yet."

Jane noticed a look flicker across Robin's face. Not quite able to read it, Jane considered asking the woman what she was thinking.

"I find it difficult to believe that Hezbollah would back down from anyone," Daniel interjected.

"Only because secrecy is still their primary objective. They're putting pieces in place – they aren't quite ready to wage their war," Atlas explained.

"Am I the only one bothered by the notion that they're putting pieces in place?" Alex raised a hand to interrupt.

"Those of us in unofficial channels are quite bothered by it," Atlas quickly assured her. "Those in more official capacities are either oblivious or unsure how to respond to it."

"What were you thinking a moment ago, Robin?" Jane couldn't resist asking any longer. "When Atlas was telling us his plan… what were you thinking?"

"It's nothing." Robin waved her off.

"Robin doesn't approve of bombing narcotics factories," Atlas supplied.

"That must put you in a difficult position then, given your line of work." Devon studied the young woman closely. Jane could tell he was trying to decide what to make of her.

"It's not the narcotics factories themselves I'm opposed to bombing. It's the slaves inside them, given that many of them started out as foster children in the United States."

CHAPTER NINETEEN

DEVON HAD HEARD RUMORS BEFORE, rumors about American children finding themselves in the red light district in Tijuana before landing in narcotics factories in Mexico. Never would he have imagined that those rumors were not only true, but that such a vast evil had found its way to his backyard.

Long after the conversation had wound down, the operatives had left, and his guests had gone to bed, he sat alone on his patio, staring into the night and wondering what to do, if anything, about Robin's revelation. To alter their plans wouldn't change the plight of these lost children. It might lengthen the term of their imprisonment, but it would do nothing to save them. They'd still end up in a landfill when they'd served their purpose.

But to move ahead with Atlas's plan meant the possible murder of innocent teenagers. Or rather, it meant the definite killing of teenagers who were most likely innocent. Because the reality was they had no way of knowing with any certainty that the workers were innocent. He supposed some might look like they weren't from Ecuador, but what about the Eduardos in the group? He could no more imagine killing Eduardo than he could a child smuggled down from the States.

Devon felt Jane's presence before she spoke, but he waited for her to make herself known. She settled into the seat beside him, joining in his reverie for a few moments before finally slicing through the quiet with her gentle voice. "I like Eduardo. He seems like a good kid."

"I think he's in love with you," Devon chuckled. "But then, there seems to be a rash of that lately."

"Very funny." Jane didn't know exactly how to respond to that. "It was very kind of him to risk his life to save us. The Eduardos of the world give me hope."

"That they do." Devon absentmindedly traced his fingers along the back of Jane's hand, marveling at how delicate it was.

"It hardly seems fair, does it? I mean, it was one thing to have this big, bad guy standing between me and the preserve, but at least we had a plan. Things were clear cut, black and white."

"We picked up a few shades of gray tonight, didn't we?"

She bit her lip for a moment before responding. "Maybe. Or maybe the right answer is still clear; it just got a whole lot more inconvenient."

"When you put it that way, I guess we don't have much of a choice." Devon tried to give her an encouraging smile.

"We're going to try to help those kids, right?" She turned imploring eyes to him.

"What will we do with a basement full of kids who've been horrifically abused for over half of their lives?"

"But we're going to try to help those kids, right?" Jane persisted.

Devon heaved a weary sigh. "Yeah, we're going to try to help those kids."

"Thank you." Jane threw her arms around his neck and kissed his cheek. When she moved to reclaim her seat, his arms wrapped around her, pulling her onto his lap.

"I'm not ready to let you go yet." He nuzzled her neck.

"What happened to giving me space?" Despite her words, her body relaxed into him.

"If space is what you want, you can have it – tomorrow."

Jane nodded silently. It made Devon inordinately happy to simply exist in the same space as her for that stolen moment. The rise and fall of her chest, the feel of her in his arms, her soft, feminine scent, they all brought comfort.

"Tomorrow maybe I can start looking for a rescue center that might have room," Jane suggested.

"Finding one with room will be a trick. It might also be difficult to accomplish much over the Internet."

"Do you think your Internet use is being tracked?"

"Possibly, but I doubt it. I have a pretty secure system. I just don't know how many resources are out there, and if they exist, I doubt they have an online presence."

"Then what do you recommend?"

"Hear me out," Devon hesitated.

"That doesn't bode well."

"I think you should take Cassandra into Quito." As soon as his words registered, Jane sat straight up and would have shot off his lap if he hadn't tightened his grip. "She knows everybody who's anybody. If someone could dig up a place for these kids to go, it would be her."

"How can I be sure she won't ditch me? What if she leaves me beside the road like a puppy nobody wants?"

"She won't abandon or hurt you." Devon tucked away the smile he felt surfacing. He didn't imagine Jane would appreciate it.

"How can you be so sure?"

"For one, I do think she's truly sorry for her actions and is looking for a way to redeem herself. For another, she's smart enough to know that if she wants a severance package out of me, she'll have to return you unscathed."

"Can you imagine how tense the car ride will be?" Jane was yielding. He could feel it in her body language, hear it in her voice. More than the errand itself, Devon was glad she was agreeing because it would get her out of town before the raid on Barrera's compound.

"If it makes you feel any better, I'll be sending someone from my security team with you."

"I'm not sure that does make me feel better," Jane pouted. "Sure, that means Cassandra has to be on her best behavior, but it means I do, too."

Devon chuckled. "Is that a bad thing?"

"I still kind of want to punch her."

"Mercy – remember mercy."

"What I'm going to remember is you throwing this mercy thing in my face," Jane threatened. "One day, that's going to come back to bite you in the butt."

"Duly noted." Devon did his best to look solemn. "Do you want me to talk to Cass or not?"

"Fine. Talk to her. I can't promise it'll go well, though." Jane crossed her arms defiantly. "And you don't have to send a security guard to babysit. I'll behave, I promise."

Devon bit back the "You're welcome" he wanted to tease her with. Instead, he chose to enjoy the silence that descended anew.

The next day was an exhausting one for Devon. Once he saw Cass and Jane off on their thinly veiled shopping trip – and said a little prayer to whomever might be inclined to listen that they wouldn't kill each other – he turned his attention to Alex. He felt like he'd wasted so much of her and her family's visit, not that any of it could have been helped. He wished they could have a week to just be together, though. Preferably a week with Jane at his side, as a couple, so he wouldn't waste that week pining for her, too. Though it galled Devon to admit pining for anyone or anything.

While Alex packed her family's belongings, Devon sat in the middle of the floor playing with his niece and nephew. As he tickled the babies, he decided there was no better sound in the world than a child in a fit of giggles.

"You'd better not make them laugh so hard they throw up."

"That's pleasant." Devon wrinkled his nose.

"I know. That's why I don't want you to do it. They just ate."

"Spoil sport," Devon accused in a silly voice, making an equally absurd face. The twins giggled again.

"So how many children do you and Jane want? When you wear her down, I mean."

"Wear her down? That sounds horrible. I prefer to think of it as winning her heart."

"Do you remember how much crap you gave Daniel for sounding all moony over me? You are such a hypocrite."

"No. This is totally different. You're my sister. This is Jane."

"Nice." She threw a pillow at him.

"Hey. Watch the kiddos. What kind of mom are you?"

Alex responded by leaning over and popping him on the back of the head with her hand. "Is that better?"

"Much."

"Great. Now stop dodging the question. I think you two would be amazing parents."

Devon focused even harder on the twins, not looking his sister in the eye as he answered. "Jane can't have children."

"I know, and that's awful, it truly is, but I assumed you'd be thinking about adoption. Or maybe even buying a medical miracle or something. It's not like you to just accept something as suckish as that."

"You're right. I think there's just so much going on at the moment I hadn't even stopped to think about it." He leaned back against the bed and thought for a moment. "I guess it just depends on what Jane wants. I'd have a houseful. This place always seems so empty when you leave. I usually throw myself into work for a week or two until I don't notice anymore, but I'm struggling more and more to care about McAlister."

"I think we should find someone to take over some of those duties." Alex came to sit on the bed near Devon. He leaned against her legs and she ruffled his hair.

"That would be nice." More and more, Devon knew he had to get out from under some of his McAlister responsibilities if he ever intended to have a life outside of work. "The only person I can think of who is qualified just demolished my trust in her, though."

"What about all that mercy crap you were telling Jane to remember?" Alex nudged his shoulder.

"Mercy crap? You are a horrible person sometimes."

"Whatever. Stop deflecting."

"There's a difference between mercy and stupidity. Cass made a colossal error in judgment," Devon reminded his sister.

"She did, but at least you know she has it out of the way. Nobody's perfect. That's one mistake in how many years, fifteen? She was bound to make one eventually," Alex shrugged. "Watch her like a hawk for six months then turn her loose. What's the worst that could happen?"

"She'll crash the company and thousands of workers will be out of a job?"

"Well, there's that. But I don't think she'll crash it. She's loyal to a fault. If anything, you'll want to make it abundantly clear that ethics should always be a priority in her business decisions."

"I'll think about it," Devon conceded, realizing he really would think about it. "You know, I'm going to miss you like crazy when you're gone."

"I know you will." She patted him on the head. "But that just means you have to bring Jane to visit us in Tuwanga. Soon."

"Admit it; you'll miss me, too."

"Maybe a little. Come on; help me clean the twins up before their nap."

Bathing and changing Erena and Joseph was a wholly messy affair, and it made Devon reconsider his proclamation that he'd have a houseful. Maybe one or two was a better number. The rest of the day passed more quickly than Devon wanted it to. Before he was ready, he and Daniel were sitting in the study arguing with Atlas about how best to proceed.

"Absolutely not. It's too risky," Atlas decreed as if he was used to that being the end of the conversation.

"Yes, it's risky, but that doesn't mean the safer path is the right one. How can you in good conscience kill innocent children?" Daniel argued.

"At this stage, they are anything but innocent."

"Is that their fault?" Devon asked.

"Fault doesn't make much difference. You're still suggesting I risk my life and that of my team to turn a drug-addicted teenager loose on society – one who has undergone enough torture to turn even the most trained soldier's mind to mush," Atlas argued. "I just don't see how that's in anybody's best interest."

"I'm not suggesting you do it. Just get me in there. I'll take the risk. I'll try to get them out while you do your thing," Devon persuaded.

"You mean *we* will," Daniel interjected.

"I can't ask that of you."

"You didn't ask. I'm volunteering. Alex and I talked about it – she's taking the kids home and I'm staying behind a couple of days. You aren't in this alone."

If Devon hadn't been in a room full of people, he might have teared up a little at Daniel's speech. There were no words to adequately express his thanks.

Atlas interrupted their exchange. "This is very touching, truly, but I'm not okay with the two of you traipsing through the middle of my operation."

"Then we'll move tonight so we're out before your operation," Daniel countered.

"Do you even know where they're keeping their slaves? Do you have any idea who is a slave and who isn't?"

Devon answered that one. "Not off the top of my head, no. And I was rather hoping you'd help answer some of those questions, but if we have to go it alone, we will. I can't not try."

Atlas opened his mouth to retort but Robin interrupted. "I'll help you."

"You'll be defying orders if you do." Atlas's tone was cool.

"Yeah, well, this is my last mission anyway. The lines between good guys and bad guys are getting awfully blurry these days."

"What's that supposed to mean?"

"It means we've outlived our usefulness. I give it six months until we're being hunted down like dogs because they can't control us. It means I'm tired of the drug lords being cut deals but the slaves in the factories being blown to bits. I'm done. I'm only here because I wanted to help this lady get her jaguar preserve back," Robin explained.

"That would have been good to know." Irritation seethed from Atlas.

"You know you can count on me tomorrow. I'm not gone yet. But we have to give these guys a map and a fifteen-minute head start to see if they can save even one innocent person first. That's all I'm saying."

Robin's impassioned speech seemed to have no effect on Atlas. Devon and Daniel exchanged glances, wondering what they'd stumbled into.

"I'll give you a map and ten minutes. Move fast or die with them." Atlas's tone was completely flat, leaving Devon to believe he meant what he said.

"Do you have kids, Mr. Atlas? Because I bet you were a real warm and fuzzy kind of dad if so." Devon knew he should sound more grateful, but he couldn't help getting at least one barb in.

Atlas merely arched an eyebrow. Devon assumed the expression meant the man wasn't amused.

CHAPTER TWENTY

"YOU KNOW I'M JUST BABYSITTING YOU to keep you from getting killed, right?" Cass asked point-blank, her eyes leaving the road long enough to cut over to Jane. "He's counting on these hellish Ecuadorian roads to keep you busy for a few days."

"Don't sugarcoat it, sweetie. Tell me how you really feel," Jane muttered.

"I'm sorry, what do you want from me?"

"A spark of humanity would be nice." Jane's reply was deadpan.

"Wow."

"Well?" Jane threw her hands up in exasperation. It was going to be a long ride. Maybe she should have taken Devon up on the offer of a security guard after all. At least he would have given her someone to talk to.

After a moment of silent fuming, Cass replied. "I have no desire to be your friend."

"I'm not suggesting we become besties. Just that we could maybe set aside our differences for a common good."

Cass's tone was derisive. "I told you, this is a babysitting mission and nothing more."

"First of all, I refuse to believe that." Jane folded her arms across her chest. She sincerely wished Cass would stop being such a heifer. "Second, even if that was the case, Devon's not here. He can't stop us from being productive. He said you were well-connected, that you would know where to start looking for help. So how about you un-bunch your panties and help?"

"Un-bunch my panties?" Cass repeated, incredulous.

"It's just a saying," Jane snapped. "I don't really care what's going on with your panties."

"That's classy."

"When I'm angry, my Southern redneck seeps out a bit. It's your fault, really."

"Does Devon know this about you?"

"You do realize that even if I left tomorrow, it still wouldn't happen between you and Devon, right?" The instant the words left her mouth, Jane regretted them. She hadn't intended to hurt Cass, and she could see that she had.

What she didn't expect was for Cass to slam on the brakes and throw the car into park. "That's it. I'm done."

Jane watched the enraged woman get out of the car. She stood in the middle of the pock-marked dirt road and glared at Jane belligerently.

"Are you waiting for me to come fight you?" Jane slowly got out of the car. "Because I think that would be counterproductive."

"On the contrary, the only way I think I'll ever be able to focus on anything other than punching that pretty little face of yours is if I punch that pretty little face of yours."

Jane blinked. She'd never been in a fistfight before. This was definitely a first for her. She straightened her shoulders and walked over to Cass as regally as she knew how. "Trust me; I've envisioned hitting you plenty of times, even though I'm kind of appalled at myself for it. But this is stupid. Are we really going to roll around in the dirt fighting over a guy when we're supposed to be on a mission to help slaves find a safe house? Really?"

"When you put it that way...." Cass seemed to contemplate Jane's words, so it took Jane totally by surprise when the petite blonde took a swing at her.

Jane grabbed her cheek in shock. "That hurt."

"I don't know; I feel better now." Cass's smile was one of satisfaction.

"Well, peachy for you." Jane hauled off and punched Cass in the nose with every ounce of strength she possessed.

"You bitch," Cass accused.

"Likewise," Jane retaliated.

The two women lunged at each other, toppling to the ground in a heap of blond hair and furious grappling. By the time it became evident to Jane that neither of them was getting the upper hand, both women were panting from the exertion. Like two young elk with horns locked to the death, they held on to each other, each refusing to let the other go.

"This is doing nothing to help those kids." Jane ground the words out.

"Then let go." Cass's reply was equally strained.

"You."

"Doubt it."

"Oh, fine." Jane relented. The release of pressure took Cass so by surprise that the woman rolled into Jane. Warily, they rose to their feet. Jane tried in vain to dust herself off and straighten her hair. She could tell by her reflection in the car window that she was a hopeless mess. Everything hurt. She could see the beginnings of a black eye, and blood trickled from her nose and the side of her lip. She decided right then there was a good reason she'd never been in a brawl before.

"You look like hell." Cass's giggle surprised them both.

"I might need a few days before I can laugh about this." Jane tried to scowl but it hurt too badly.

Cass giggled all the harder. "I'm sorry. I don't know what came over me."

"Just as long as you've got it out of your system," Jane sighed.

"Do you?"

"Yeah. I don't think I was meant to be a fighter."

"There are different kinds of fighters." Cass fired the car back to life. "Let's go see if we can do some productive fighting."

"I don't suppose we could stop somewhere to get some new clothes and clean up first?" Jane tenderly touched her eye. "There's not much we can do to hide the black eyes, but we might get a better response if we don't look like we're in need of a safe house ourselves."

"Sure. We'll use Devon's credit card since this is all really his fault anyway. Wait, I have a black eye?" Cass leaned over to check her reflection in the mirror. "Well, crap."

At that, Jane did giggle.

CHAPTER
TWENTY-ONE

DEVON CHECKED HIS WATCH; five minutes until he and Daniel were a go. His stomach was in knots, but he kept his expression impassive. As his eyes scanned the horizon for potential threats, his mind wandered back to the new instructions he'd finalized with his lawyer just moments before heading out. A smile tugged the corner of his lips at the thought of Jane and Cass trying to coexist to run his estate. Poor Alex would be so mad at him for thrusting her in the middle of that mess.

He'd heard that a person's life flashed before their eyes just before death. All Devon could think about was Jane. The moments that flashed through his mind all centered on her. From first laying eyes on her at the village marketplace, to working up the nerve to say hello; finding her on his property, staring up a tree; all the way up to holding her in his arms, feeling like nothing else in the world could possibly be more right.

Devon glanced at his watch again. It was time. He exchanged one last look with Daniel, hoping his friend understood how very much his being there meant to Devon. He resolved to do whatever was necessary to be sure his brother-in-law made it back to Alex in one piece. Of course, with Daniel's military background, he probably stood a better chance than Devon did with his corporate experience.

Trusting that Atlas had been able to block them from Barrera's security system and Pablo had temporarily disabled Devon's, the two men scaled the fence and made their way through the jungle to the coordinates they'd been given for the underground factory. As they neared their goal, they encountered their first guard. Daniel disposed of the man before he could radio in the threat, reminding Devon once again just how well-trained his friend was.

It took them a moment to find the door to the factory. The longer the search drew out, the more nervous Devon got. They'd used their ten minutes. Drug enforcement agents – both official and not – would be converging on Barrera's operation by now.

Sweat covered Devon's brow by the time he heaved the door open. Shots rang out the instant sunlight hit the dank cellar. Devon jumped back, but not before a bullet brushed his thigh. He swore under his breath.

"I'm not here to hurt you," he shouted from behind the tree he'd taken as cover.

"Unless you keep shooting," Daniel amended.

"If you are here against your will, come with me now, and I'll see that you make it to safety." Devon felt a little foolish. Maybe Atlas had been right. Maybe bombing the bunker would have made more sense. It certainly would have been easier.

"You have to the count of three to decide if you belong to Javier Barrera or if you want to be a free man," Daniel called out. "One. Two...."

A female voice rose above the chaos that erupted. "I'm coming out."

At her pronouncement, all hell broke loose. Daniel and Devon tried to peer into the hole, then looked back at each other. Devon wondered if anyone would survive their rescue attempt. He mouthed at Daniel, "Wait here."

He cautiously approached the hole again, his gun ready. It was probably suicide, but he had to try to go in after the girl. He was met by a man with a gun leveled on him; without thinking, Devon pulled his own trigger. The gunman fell, only to be replaced by another.

That one was taken out by Daniel. "I'll do my best to cover you."

Devon nodded, swallowing hard before descending the steps into the unknown. He counted it no small miracle when his feet touched the ground without being shot at again. He turned a circle to verify there wasn't a gun pointed at his back.

In addition to the two guards he and Daniel had felled, another was sprawled on the ground, an apparent victim of a coup. Other bodies scattered the room as well. Devon tried not to think about how many died without seeing freedom. Instead, he focused on the lone remaining guard standing behind a filthy young woman, a gun held to her temple.

"Back off, *gringo*. Just get out of here," the frightened man ordered.

"You and I both know you're going to shoot her whether I leave or not," Devon stated calmly.

"Do you want to watch her die?"

"No." Devon shook his head slowly, waiting for his opportunity. "But I can't say I'll mind watching you die."

Seizing his brief window, Devon took aim and fired, hitting the man right in the middle of his forehead. As he fell backwards, the girl was pulled off balance. A boy next to her reached out to set her right again.

There were maybe a dozen frightened pairs of eyes scattered throughout the vast underground factory, all watching him expectantly. Devon gave what he hoped was a reassuring smile.

"Is this everybody?" he asked.

The girl nodded, stepping to the front of the group.

"Okay, then. My partner is waiting for you at the top of the stairs. He'll take the lead; I'll take the rear. We have to move quickly. This place is probably already under attack."

As if to remove any doubt, the ground shook from an explosion in the distance.

"Now might be a really good time to get out of here," Daniel called down.

"You heard him." Devon motioned for them to head to the stairs. Again, it was the young woman who led the way. Devon admired her courage.

The trip up the stairs seemed to take even longer than the one down had. When Devon emerged, it was to find the world around him aflame. He realized with sickening clarity that they were in the middle of a war zone. While it seemed nobody was around to fire directly on them or even care as they picked their way back through the jungle, the odds of being caught in the crossfire were pretty good and increasing by the moment.

The girl who'd led the others out of the abyss fell and twisted her ankle. Without breaking stride, Daniel backtracked long enough to scoop her up. Devon knew they were hungry, tired and dazed, but he urged them to move faster.

When they reached the fence between Barrera's compound and his own plantation, it was obvious the beleaguered captives would never be able to make the climb, so he cut the fence and held it aside for them to crawl through.

Devon hoped his fence's security alarm had been turned back on. If it had, cutting it would have triggered a silent alarm, which would mean a security guard would be on his way to check things out. Until he arrived, the ragtag little group trudged on. Devon couldn't help wondering if Jane had been successful in finding a safe house or if he'd just strapped on a whole lot more than he knew what to do with.

His leg throbbed, reminding him he'd been nicked by a bullet. Still, he was shocked and immensely grateful it was only minor. Even better, he was bringing Daniel back in one piece. He'd never have forgiven himself if he'd been responsible for making his sister a young widow.

It bothered him not knowing what had gone on with the raid. Judging from the chaos, he'd failed to grasp the extent of the strike. If their luck held, then maybe the security cameras went down before he and Daniel made their trek across Javier's property. Ideally, he'd never connect them to what happened today and there would be no retaliation on Devon or his plantation. There were so many innocent people on that plantation who had nothing to do with the mess happening next door.

It felt like a lifetime passed before the lone security guard showed up. Devon gave his employee the benefit of the doubt that it hadn't actually been that long. He loaded the weakest rescues in the vehicle and sent the guard back with instructions to radio in for someone else to come out right away. It wasn't long before Pablo answered the call in his pickup truck. Again, Devon loaded the weakest of their group in the cab; then he and Daniel climbed in the back of the truck with the rest.

He closed his eyes and enjoyed the feel of the wind bathing his face on the bumpy ride back, wondering if this could really be the conclusion of their trouble with Javier Barrera. After all of the planning and waiting, to have it simply end in one quick swoop seemed almost too good to be true.

Once they unloaded the refugees, Lucia set to cooking for them while Pablo helped them process through showering. He sent another staff member out to round up extra clothing since their new guests were wearing little better than rags.

Devon quietly retreated to his own master suite to shower and doctor his leg. Once he was dressed and feeling almost human again, he called Jane to check in.

"Oh, thank God." Jane's relief was obvious. He couldn't be sure, but it almost sounded like she was crying. "I was so scared for you. Did you get them?"

"Not all." The image of bodies littering the floor flashed through his mind. "But we saved some."

"Some is better than none. It's everything to the ones you did get."

"I needed that reminder. Thank you." Devon rested his forehead against the wall and tried to picture Jane as they spoke. She was the focal point grounding him, keeping him moving forward.

"How many?"

"A dozen. Young men and women. All of them are hungry and scared. They've barely said two words. I'm not sure how well they speak English, although two-thirds of them don't look like they're from around here."

"The poor things."

"Have you had any luck? Do we have somewhere for them to go?" Devon had visions of his house being overrun with refugees indefinitely and instantly felt selfish for cringing at the prospect. From the tone of Jane's voice, he wouldn't put it past her to take them all under her wing without batting an eyelash.

"I just stepped out of a meeting Cass was able to arrange. I hate to ask you to just get your checkbook out, but are you willing to make a donation to the organization that takes them in?"

"Whatever it takes."

"I don't know. They're asking for a lot of money." Jane was hesitant.

"Does Cass trust them to use the money for the kids?"

"She does."

"Then whatever it takes," he reiterated.

Devon could hear the smile in her voice when she responded. "You're a good man, Devon McAlister. Do you know that?"

He chuckled. "You're going to make me blush."

"I wish I could see that."

"I miss you." The need to be with her was overwhelming.

Her voice softened. "I miss you, too. Maybe you could come with the kids?"

There was such hesitation in her voice when she offered the suggestion. He had the distinct impression she still didn't fully understand that he'd walk through the fires of hell for her. She had no clue how precious she was to him.

"If you think they have somewhere to go when we get there, we'll leave as soon as they've eaten. I'd prefer Javier not find his missing workers camped out in my living room. I don't want to bring the wrath of Hezbollah down on my employees. And I will most definitely accompany them. If I don't get you in my arms soon, I just might go a little crazy."

Jane laughed softly in response. "We wouldn't want that. But yes, you'll have somewhere for them. Your checkbook and Cass's tenacity are a magical combination. You really should put her in charge of your U.S. operations so you can take a step back."

Devon blinked and held the phone out to look at it, wondering what parallel universe he'd stepped into.

"I'm thinking about it" was all he'd commit to. "I'll call you when we're on our way."

As he hung up the phone and went to see if he could help Pablo, Devon had to admit to himself he was mildly afraid of the prospect of Cass and Jane cooperating.

CHAPTER
TWENTY-TWO

"I DON'T THINK I WANT TO KNOW." Devon surveyed Jane and Cass's injuries as he climbed out of his Jeep. "No, actually, I am kind of curious. Was it a barroom brawl? Attacked by pirates? Marauding bears, maybe?"

Jane watched his lip twitch and she knew he was wrestling with a smile. "Lucky for you, I'm happy to see you alive, so I won't tell you how rude it is to laugh at people."

"But I'm not laughing. In fact, I think I'm doing a pretty admirable job at not laughing. I'm doing a much better job than Pablo." Devon pointed to his friend, who was openly chuckling in his truck.

One look from Cass stifled Pablo's amusement.

"It's probably best to leave it to your imagination." Jane decided. "Are we going to get these refugees inside, or do you want to keep digging a hole for yourself?"

"I'm telling myself there was mud involved. Or Jell-O."

Cass pinned Devon with a withering glare.

"You girls can tell me about it later."

Jane let his amusement roll off her. Cass didn't look quite so inclined. For Jane, it was all she could do to not publicly humiliate herself by clinging to Devon now that he was in her sight. She knew at any moment the adrenaline of the day would wear off and she'd be little better than a puddle on the floor. Somehow, though, she managed to hold herself together while they got the refugees settled and even on the way back to the hotel.

Devon had called ahead to arrange hotel rooms for the four of them, though on three separate floors. Jane was the first to get off the elevator with a meek "goodnight" and a longing look back at Devon. She wanted to hear the details of the raid. She wanted to fill him in on her newfound truce with Cass. She wanted to curl up in his arms and listen to the steady beat of his heart telling her everything was going to be okay now.

Instead, because she'd asked him for space, she trudged down the hall to her room alone. After struggling with her key for a moment, she let herself in, stopping short as the door swung closed behind her. Her room was aglow with soft candlelight. A bouquet of red roses sat on a small table. Jane paused to take in their rich fragrance before following a trail of rose petals that led to the bathroom, where she found a hot bath waiting and her new satin and lace pajama set laid out for her.

As lovely as a nice long soak in a hot tub sounded, Jane didn't trust herself not to fall asleep. She'd thank Devon for his kind gesture in the morning; he didn't need to know she'd washed quickly and hopped into bed.

When Jane went to turn down her covers, she found another rose. This time it was one of the flowers he'd named after her. Everything in Jane wanted to find Devon, to spend the night in his arms. She couldn't say what held her back; she didn't know. All she knew was that drifting off to sleep with her rose on the nightstand seemed a poor substitute for the real thing.

Over the next several days, the ache in Jane's heart only increased. Devon's discomfort over her newfound friendship with Cass provided the levity that kept her from completely climbing a wall. Every time Jane and Cass would giggle over a shared joke, usually when they'd catch a glimpse of the other's bruising, it would send Devon skittering sideways as if he was dealing with an unknown wild animal. His reaction would make them laugh all the harder.

It was kind of crazy how well their roadside brawl had ended tensions between them. However it came about, Jane embraced their truce and Cass's help. The tiny woman was a force of nature. Even so, it took her days of holing up in the office with Devon for the two of them to get the McAlister workload back under control.

It was while Devon and Cass were elbow-deep in fiscal reports that Robin showed up on Devon's doorstep with the first news of the raid. Jane showed the beleaguered woman to the receiving room and asked Lucia to bring some refreshments for their guest.

When Jane mentioned calling Devon down, Robin interrupted. "Don't bother him. I can't stay long. Nobody knows I'm here and I'd prefer to keep it that way. Cody is on his way down to update you in person. He's pretty uptight about using unsecured phones, and visits can be passed off as business because of the work he does with McAlister."

"Oh." Jane tried to process what Robin was telling her. "Why don't you want them to know you're here?"

"I'm getting out. I joined Chameleon to make a difference; I thought I was doing something good. Now, I'm not so sure."

"Chameleon?" Jane struggled to keep up. "Is that the name of the organization you and Atlas work for?"

Robin nodded, blinking back the tears that sprang to her eyes. "Atlas... Atlas didn't make it out. I think they killed him. Javier is gone, though. The house is empty; the factory is destroyed. All that's left are the bodies. Most of his people aren't accounted for, so I think they've pulled back to regroup. I just don't know where. If I knew where, I'd go try to find him, to be sure."

"Be sure?"

"We haven't found Atlas's body. There's a chance they've taken him prisoner." Robin closed her eyes, her brow furrowed in pain. "What if they're torturing him? Barrera has to be desperate to find out what Atlas knows."

Jane's own stomach clenched at the thought. Maybe Atlas hadn't been the most pleasant person she'd ever met, but he'd put his life on the line to root out the nest of vipers in her backyard. It shook Jane to her core to think of any man being tortured, but knowing he'd been captured while helping her made it all the worse.

"Can I do anything to help you?" Jane wondered. "Where will you go now?"

Robin smiled at her. "I don't need anything, thank you. I think I'll go see if I can help the world another way. I'm not cut out for the intrigue of this particular path."

"Thank you for coming by, for telling us what happened." Jane couldn't stop thinking about Atlas.

"It should be safe to go home now."

Jane sat up a little straighter. Home was something she hadn't thought about in a few days, maybe more. She was eager to go back, to start again with the jaguars. Still, she couldn't help wondering what that meant for her and Devon.

Most likely oblivious to the tumult going on in Jane's head, Robin continued, "I have to warn you, it's a mess. You have fences to repair, and your buildings have been all but leveled. I'm so sorry."

"It's okay," Jane quickly reassured her. "I mean, not okay, but you know what I mean. What's done is done. There's nothing to do about it now but rebuild. I have to have faith that even something as terrible as all of this can be used for good. I'll just cling to that until I figure out what it is."

"I admire you for that. Right now, I'm struggling to see it."

Robin looked so very sad that Jane couldn't help hugging her. "I'm struggling to see it, too," she admitted.

Jane couldn't say why, but she didn't tell Devon about Robin's visit right away. She told herself it was because she didn't want to bother him while he was working. Cody would arrive soon enough with news.

He showed up that evening while they were eating dinner. As Lucia set another place, Cody quickly and quietly filled them in on everything he knew. Hearing Atlas had been captured was only slightly less of a punch in the gut the second time.

"The good news," Cody finally smiled, "is that Jane can go home. We have no idea where they've gone, and I would highly recommend installing a security system, but she can go home and start rebuilding."

Jane's return smile lacked enthusiasm. Her hope that nobody would notice vanished when Devon arched a neat eyebrow at her. She read the expression on his face well enough to know he was curious about her reaction. He didn't say anything, though. Jane breathed a sigh of relief when he merely played along with the conversation.

By the time she'd showered and dressed for bed, she was soul-weary. She felt like an old woman who'd seen and done too much, who knew too many of the world's secrets. Jane wasn't sure she could ever feel safe in this world again.

She answered the tap at her door, melting with relief when she saw Devon standing on the other side of it. Without a word, he pushed her through the entrance and up against the wall. When his mouth claimed hers, she could feel the urgency radiating from him. She pulled him deeper into her, meeting his need with her own.

Just as Jane approached the point of no return, the moment when she knew she would beg him for more, he ended the kiss, resting his head against hers, his arms still planted on either side of her.

"Remember when I promised to give you space?" He was breathless.

Jane gulped air into her own lungs before replying, "Vividly."

"I think I lied. No, I'm certain of it."

"That's okay. Space is overrated."

He grinned at her response before kissing her again. This time his touch held more than desire; it held promise.

His sandpaper jaw grazed her skin as the warmth of his mouth blazed a trail of fire across her collarbone. Jane closed her eyes, relishing the sensation as he moved on to her neck. She struggled to breathe as his simple exploration drew her into a spiraling vortex of pleasure.

Jane couldn't say exactly what or when it happened, but as she returned the attention, as she sought to please him, to be even closer to him, the last vestiges of her defensive barriers crumbled. She knew in her heart that she was wholly his, for better or for worse.

It wasn't until later, lying wrapped in his arms and basking in the glow of his love, that she brought up Robin's earlier visit. He listened quietly as she filled him in on the conversation the two women had shared.

"I wondered why you didn't look surprised earlier." Realization dawned in Devon's voice. "Although, I'm not sure that's all I saw in your face. What aren't you telling me?"

Jane didn't answer. There was no graceful way to admit she didn't want to go home anymore; that somehow over these past few weeks she'd come to think of the plantation as home. She couldn't exactly invite herself over. Camping out in his backyard would probably be frowned on.

"Aw, come on," Devon persisted. "It's not fair keeping secrets from me. I know there's something bumping around your brain right now. What is it?"

Jane took a deep breath before taking the plunge. "I was just thinking about how much I'm going to miss you, how much I'm going to miss your home. You've been very good to me... to all of us. You are truly a good man, Devon."

"You don't have to leave, you know," Devon spoke cautiously as his hand stroked the small of her back.

"Devon...." Jane began to protest.

"I'm not talking sleepovers," he cut off her reply. "I was kind of hoping, since we'll be spending so much time together rebuilding the preserve, that somewhere in all of that togetherness I'd be able to convince you to come back on a more permanent basis."

Jane didn't answer; she didn't trust herself not to say something stupid. She was too happy for her brain's filter to function properly.

"Jane?" Devon prompted. "You're not supposed to leave a guy hanging once he's put himself out there like that. It's not nice."

She propped herself up to look down into Devon's eyes. The candle on her bedside table flickered, lending to the magic of the moment. She could see the love shining on his face – it was there to plainly see. Her heart was bursting with love for this confident, amazing man who'd made himself so vulnerable at her feet. Jane smiled and touched the dimple that appeared when he returned her smile. "I was just thinking that I look forward to you trying to persuade me."

EPILOGUE

DEVON CLOSED HIS EYES, basking in the sun's warmth and enjoying the feel of the waves lapping at his feet and legs. Jane's fingers were woven into his, her gentle presence at his side making the moment all the more delectable.

"Your sister's home is amazing," Jane said, breaking the easy silence between them. "This was a perfect suggestion for our honeymoon."

"You made Alex a very happy woman by agreeing to that suggestion," Devon murmured, in a happy state of not quite awake.

"Do you ever get used to the fact that you're staying in the royal palace, though?" Jane wondered aloud. "I want to be royalty."

"You'll have to settle for being in-laws with royalty. I'm sorry; you married plain ole' me."

Jane laughed at that. "There is nothing plain about you."

"Nor you, Mrs. McAlister."

Jane took a deep breath as if to reply but simply sighed instead. "Thank you for loving me, for all of this."

Devon opened his eyes and looked at his wife. As always, he was totally in awe of her beauty. The South Pacific agreed with her. Her newly tanned skin glistened in the sunlight. Her hair, lightened even more by their time here, tumbled about her like a heavenly halo. He pulled her into his arms and sighed. "You still don't get it, do you?"

"Get what?"

"How thankful I am for every single day I wake up with you at my side. I look at you and am completely overwhelmed by the fact that you're mine. You're everything to me."

A giggle erupted in the distance. Jane and Devon both turned their heads to watch in amusement as Alex chased the pair of gleefully squealing toddlers across the beach, calling to Eduardo for reinforcements when they split up and took diverging paths. If Devon didn't know any better, he'd think they'd planned that so at least one of them had a better chance of making a break for it.

"I'm sorry I can't give you that someday." There was an unmistakable sadness in her voice.

"I'm sorry too, but only because I think the world would be a better place if there were more of you in it." Devon stroked her hair and searched for the exact words he wanted. "But have you given any thought at all to our other options?"

"Have you?"

Devon had been giving it a great deal of thought, actually. "If you really want to try to find a way to have our own child, I'll support that decision. But I think I'd really like to look into adopting. I mean, more than the sixteen-year-old we seem to have inherited. There are just so many children who need a family. Think of the difference we could make to a child."

"Eduardo's a pretty good place to start. I mean, he did save my life, and the hard work is pretty much done." Jane's eyes followed the boy for a moment before turning back to Devon. "Just one?"

"Actually, I'd like a lot more than one, but I didn't want to mentally commit until we'd talked," Devon admitted.

"Most people talk about this kind of thing before they get married, you know." She toyed with a stray strand of hair.

"Yeah, well, why do anything the normal way?"

"I like the idea of adoption," she answered his original question. "I have no idea where to start, though."

"I'll set up some appointments for us when we get back," Devon promised.

Daniel walked up, casting a shadow over the couple. "So, uh, I hate to interrupt this little love fest and all, but I have news from Cody."

Jane sat up and shielded her eyes as she looked up at Daniel. Devon grudgingly rose and dusted the sand off his swimsuit before offering a hand to Jane.

"What does our intrepid friend from Texas have to say?" Devon wondered what couldn't have waited until his honeymoon was over.

"He just wanted to let us know they've located Javier, and Atlas is still alive. Apparently Barrera took a handful of DEA agents captive, too. Cody's sending another team in after them. Unofficially, of course."

Devon reached out to place a steadying hand on the small of Jane's back. Maybe it was an overly protective gesture, but he couldn't help it. "He told you all of this over the phone?"

"Some of us have secure phone lines," Daniel retorted.

"Makes sense." Jane shrugged.

Devon let it go. "Does he need anything from us? Is Jane safe?"

"Cody says Barrera has his hands full at the moment; he can't imagine the man is too worried about Jane – especially if word has gotten around that the two of you are married, and you know word has gotten around by now. Cody just wanted you to know. He thought you'd be able to enjoy yourselves a little more without that hanging over you."

"We can." Jane smiled. "Thank you."

"There's more news from back home," Daniel continued. "This one's a message for Jane."

"What's that?"

"Aldo just called to let you know they've confirmed it: Aria is expecting triplets." A grin broke across Daniel's face.

Jane let out a little squeal of joy and jumped into Devon's arms. His own laughter joined hers as he swung her around.

"What did I miss?" Alex joined their little group.

Devon was vaguely aware of Daniel filling her in. He didn't care what kind of audience they had; he kissed his wife, hoping he was properly able to convey just how he intended to celebrate their news once they were alone.

"Aria is going to be a mama," Jane whispered happily as she hugged his neck.

"So are you," he promised. "And you'll both be amazing mamas together."

Devon went through the rest of his day in a happy bubble. His world was fuller and richer than he could have ever imagined. That night, he and Jane made love on their balcony under the stars. With her in his arms, he felt invincible.

"Do you remember my book? The one I've been writing and writing without having any clue what it was about?" Jane asked softly as her head rested against his chest.

Devon chuckled. "I remember. I have a confession to make: I found it the day Freya died. I couldn't help reading just a little of it. So many hopes and fears tucked in the pages of such a little journal...."

"You butthead. You read my book?" She poked him in the side before moving on, not really upset. "Actually, it's funny you should say that because I was just thinking that if I ever do something with it, I want it to be a story of hope, not fear."

"Yeah?" Devon thought about her words.

"I was really scared there for a little while," she admitted. "I didn't know how my world could ever be right again. But I've decided the darkness doesn't get to win. I'm not going to let it. I'm going to enjoy this place of joy we're in now, but when the darkness returns, I'll remind myself to hope. Because if it looks like darkness is winning, that just means the story isn't over yet."

Devon thought about her words. He knew this world well enough by now to know the darkness would inevitably find them again. It always did. He liked her way of looking at it, though.

"Hope is a good theme for your book," he finally responded. "And just so we're on the same page, I intend to have a long and lovely story with you, Jane McAlister. I might not be able to stop darkness from stealing a chapter here and there, but I promise you our narrative will be filled with joy and laughter."

"Good." Jane brushed a kiss against his lips and smiled. "Because I like it when sunshine wins."

THE END

A NOTE FROM THE AUTHOR

I've written and am currently editing a book featuring Cody Kingsley from *Roses in Ecuador* in hopes of releasing it in the Spring of 2013. The title has been a source of debate; we're leaning towards *Fool's Game*, but as with any work in progress, that could change. Still, I hope you enjoy this sneak peek!

—Heather Huffman

EXCERPT FROM
FOOL'S GAME
BY HEATHER HUFFMAN

CHAPTER ONE

It was going to attack. Fear gnawed at him as his smoky eyes studied the tawny creature. Every muscle in the predator's body was tensed, ready to spring into action. A low growl emerged. The only movement was a terse flick of the animal's tail. He searched the creature's eyes for some emotion but could find none, for they were cold and black.

"As black as the damned beast's soul," he muttered; the animal's ears flicked in response. It shifted from left to right and back again then shot forward in one fluid motion. He took a hurried step back, but it was not enough. The great cat extended its powerful body and felled him with the force of a lightning bolt sent straight from the hand of God. He raised both arms in a feeble attempt to defend himself... then both man and beast halted, mesmerized.

She was there. She laughed impishly as the creature bounded towards her. He scrambled to his feet, calling out a frantic warning. She simply stood there, serene as a woman gazing at her sleeping babe. The cat stopped obediently at her feet and she knelt to scratch its ears. The animal contentedly rubbed against her legs as she stood to face him. He studied her in awe. She seemed so soft and vulnerable, making him want to hold and protect her forever; yet something inside of him also recognized the aura of power she wore as a shield.

Golden wisps of hair teased the honey skin of her shoulders. Full lips curved into a whimsical smile, and eyes of the sea seemed to mock him. He reached for her and froze. The playful light was gone from her face and he could not help but think of Poseidon in a fit of rage as he beheld the storms that flashed through her eyes.

"I don't belong to you anymore," she warned in a soft growl, turning her back to him. The magnificent cougar loped along like a faithful pet at her side as each step took her further away.

"Caitlyn," he whispered, sinking to his knees. The cougar wheeled around and lunged for him, guided by the wrath in her eyes. He dodged left...

... and found himself staring at the hardwood floor of his room.

"Damn her," he muttered, running his hands through his sun-streaked hair. Was he ever going to stop dreaming about her? Even as he asked the question, he heard the answer deep within. She would haunt him until she forgave him, because he'd destroyed and created her in one fell swoop.

*   *   *

Cat bolted upright, her feather bed suddenly made of nails. Her gaze darted nervously about the room, unsure if she was still its lone occupant. His presence had been so real.

It was this house. It always did this to her. For six years, all memories of Caitlyn O'Rourke had been tucked safely in the furthest depths of her mind, until she walked through the doors of this house. All vestiges of her past seemed so distant and unreal, except one. Damn him.

Why, after years of swearing she would hate him until the day she died, did his mere presence still wreak havoc on her brain? Even now she could feel his touch, soft as an angel's wing as it brushed her skin. She could see those eyes that always seemed to be able to penetrate her very soul. She could hear that deep, slow drawl of his.

She groaned and cuddled closer to her pillow. It had been a long night. Without rhyme or reason, she could still vividly remember his kiss, the feel of his hands spanning her waist, and his unshaven jaw as it brushed her smooth skin. She could close her eyes and that lopsided grin and forever-unruly lock of hair were hers for the taking.

She sighed, content to forget that she hated him for just a moment. If only for that moment, a world-weary soul found peace in the memory of a long-ago lover. Then reality destroyed her tranquil moment in the form of the harsh overhead light of her room.

"Does my face look orange?"

Cat transferred her glare from the pillow she was clutching to her partner, Ella. "You do realize you have to die now, don't you?"

"Dream about him again?" Ella was nonplussed as she made herself comfortable on Cat's bed.

"I don't want to talk about it." Cat frowned and changed the subject. "Your face wouldn't look orange if you didn't wear make-up that was too dark."

"That bad, huh?"

"No, but it could be better," Cat answered truthfully. That was the thing she most loved about her friendship with Ella: the brutal honesty they shared with each other. No pretense, no sugar coating. It just was what it was.

"I hate being so pale," Ella moaned. "Why can't I be tan like you?"

Cat had never understood why Ella hated her complexion so much. A lot of women would kill for her perfect alabaster skin.

"Do I look like God?" Cat arched an eyebrow. "How should I know? Why can't I be petite like you? It's just one of those little quirks of fate."

Ella went to peer into the mirror hanging over Cat's dresser. "You are such a bear in the mornings."

"Why thank you." Cat rolled over to snuggle her pillow. She could freely admit she was being a brat. She just wasn't too keen on discussing why. "I think I'll go riding this morning."

Maybe a strong horse under her and the wind in her hair would help her shake this sullen cloud she had hanging over her head.

"You have fun with that one." Ella wrinkled her nose. "I don't think horses like me very much. Of course, the feeling is kind of mutual."

"You should learn to ride." Cat found it hard to imagine that anyone could not like horses. It just didn't seem natural to her.

"Why? Because it's such a necessary part of every computer hacker's life?" Ella quipped. "Besides, some of us have work to do. My boss is a real nag, you know."

"Gee, thanks – cow," Cat slapped Ella upside the head with her pillow.

"Hussy." Ella picked up another pillow and returned the favor.

"Would you look at this abuse?" Cat asked no one in particular. "Where is my puppy to defend me when I need him?"

"Puppy? If that beast gets any bigger, I'll buy him a saddle," Ella laughed. "He went outside with Cody."

"I wish that dog would show a little discretion in his companions," Cat snorted. "Now leave, unless you want to watch me change."

"I'll be in the kitchen, sunshine." Ella saluted and strolled out the door, leaving Cat alone with her thoughts.

It was strange; the only home she knew anymore was Cody's sprawling Texas ranch. Even though Cat technically had plenty of other options, they occasionally wound up here between assignments. She'd done a good job of avoiding Cody and hadn't seen him for years – until last night.

Weary from yet another trip to Javier Barrera's fortress nestled in the jungles of Ecuador, she had completely forgotten that congress was no longer in session and Cody would be home. That is, until she nearly totaled her Mojave metallic BMW M6 Coupe because he had the audacity to leave his truck in her parking space.

Muttering an array of curses upon his head all the while, Cat had left her car as it was, grabbed her duffel bag, and hopped out of the car without bothering to wait for her companions to unfurl. Han had immediately greeted her by bathing her face in kisses as she knelt to scratch his ears. An Australian Shepherd-Border Collie hybrid, Han had been a birthday gift from Cody several years ago. She usually returned his gifts with a smart-aleck comment, but Cody knew her stubborn determination to annoy him would stop short of turning away a three-week-old pup abandoned by its mother. When he'd presented her with the tiny ball of fur, it gnawed on Cat's fingers and the bond was instantly formed.

Three years later, Han gnawed on her hand as she tried to unlock the door without the aid of light. "Cool it mutt, I'm going as fast as I can," she gently chided.

"Hey there, buddy." Han's attention was drawn from Cat by her brother and partner, Jack.

She stopped cursing Cody long enough to curse the door and all of its locks, which were placed there by Cody, so really it was all his fault either way one looked at it.

"Does he think he lives in South Central?" Cat growled. "I swear I'd have less trouble breaking into Fort Knox than I'm having opening this door with a key."

No sooner had she finished that pronouncement than the door swung open and she found herself staring into an all-too-familiar pair of blue eyes. His smirk told her he'd listened to every insult thrown at his feet as she had fought with the lock, and that irritated her beyond measure. She opened her mouth to tell him as much when it happened.

Not wanting to miss the chance to sleep inside, Han bolted past Cat, knocking her right into Cody, who instinctively caught her and wouldn't let go. It was at that moment—half standing and half kneeling with her face pressed firmly against his bare chest, her nose throbbing from the impact and unable to move as he repeated each and every descriptive term she had ever hurled his direction—Cat learned the true meaning of the word humility.

"Let go of me." His body muffled her threat. He ignored it, choosing instead to greet Jack and Ella with a cheerful hello. Driven to the brink of insanity by that, Cat somehow managed to connect the steel toe of her boot with his shin, just to let him know she was serious. He instantly dropped to the ground, moaning as if mortally wounded and unfortunately bringing her with him.

"You're not hurt that badly," she snapped while trying to free herself. Han thought it all looked like great fun and jumped right in the middle of the pile with a delighted bark. Ella and Jack had merely stepped over them and continued on to their rooms without even acknowledging Cat's accusation of being traitors.

It didn't take long for Cat to gain the upper hand and pin Cody flat on his back.

"You are mine to toy with," she mocked as Han drooled on his face. His Cheshire grin told her he had other plans, and somehow she found herself back at the bottom of the pile with both of her hands caught in one of his.

Cat wasn't sure how she'd gotten so lost in his eyes, but they stared at each other long enough to bore poor Han, who left in search of a more interesting crowd.

Cody was a beautiful man. Her gaze lingered on his lips as they formed that familiar grin, and she had to admit to herself she wanted him to kiss her. Actually, she wanted a lot more than a kiss.

That was the thought that brought her back to her senses. Cat freed herself with lightning speed, called for her dog, and high-tailed it to the relative safety of her room, cursing Cody for being so danged sexy anyway.

*   *   *

Still mulling over last night, Cat ambled down the hallway with her boots in hand.

"Do these jeans make my butt look big?" She asked no one in particular upon her entrance to the kitchen.

"No, Cat, and I really wish you'd get over this butt hang-up of yours," Ella answered as any good friend should.

Cat wasn't so sure she believed her, so she contorted her body to try to check for herself.

"You make me so proud, sis," Jack teased.

"Thank you." Cat beamed at him, choosing to pretend he meant it as she hopped around the kitchen on one leg, trying to pull her boots on.

"Cat, I thought you would realize by now that men adore us no matter what we wear," Ella jokingly reprimanded.

"Men adore you?" Jack laughed out loud. "Only if they have the IQ of a house plant."

"Most men do have the IQ of a house plant," Ella retorted.

"Now Ella, aren't you being just a little bit insulting to our house plants?" Cat smirked.

Jack made a dive for her and she easily parried. A punch was met with a kick, each move escalating the battle a little more until brother and sister mocked full-on hand-to-hand combat in the immense kitchen.

"Children, children. Please control yourselves," Ella admonished.

"Yes." Cat dodged one last kick. "Control yourself big brother." She darted out of the kitchen, her laughter lingering after.

Cat could feel her mood lifting. Ella and Jack usually had that effect on her. Her countenance further brightened when she spotted Cody's new Arabian stallion. She smiled beseechingly at the stable hand, and with a laugh he saddled the horse for her. Cody emerged from the house just as Cat and his prize new horse went sailing over the fence surrounding the inner pastures.

She took the horse at an easy trot across the outer yards and into the fields. It was there that she allowed him to open up, leaning over the animal so their bodies became one as they flew across fences and endless plains. Cody had invested wisely in the magnificent black, which seemed to have an endless supply of energy. The ground below soared past for an eternity, and still the animal kept going at an unchanging pace. She felt Cody's presence before she heard the hoof beats pounding the Texas soil. It was just like him to ruin a perfectly beautiful experience.

Realizing he was too stubborn to let up, she decided to be the mature one in the situation and slowly eased her pace. Although the stallion seemed perfectly happy to continue his run, he obediently followed her commands and was soon standing still and mimicking her angelic expression as the pair watched Cody fly by. Apparently it took him a minute to realize she'd stopped, or to get his mount to agree to do the same. Cat waited for him to turn back impatiently before she nudged her mount ahead.

"Trying to kill my new horse?" Cody asked pointedly.

"I won't dignify that with a remark." Cat sighed daintily and turned her mind to business. "I think we're ready to make a move on Barrera's compound."

"Cat," Cody hedged.

"I know what you're going to say, but I'm not moving too quickly. I know the layout of the entire place. We've got all the schematics and there are at least a dozen drug enforcement agents that have been left to rot in this guy's jails, or pits, or hell holes or whatever you want to call them...."

"Cat," he interrupted. "I don't want to say what I'm about to say, but I have to say it."

"You're rambling, Lion. Spit it out," she snapped without even realizing she had used the nickname she'd given him years ago.

"I talked to the boss. I think you know that when we got the intelligence about the prisoners, I didn't wait for clearance." He paused, unsure how to continue. "He told me to abort the mission. He has something more important."

"More important?" Cat was incredulous.

"He wants you to go to New Orleans. Your target is a man named Peyton Winthrop, a businessman with his hand in the proverbial cookie jar." Cody couldn't believe the words coming out of his mouth.

Cat took a deep breath to reign in her temper. "Two things: Since when have I become an assassin, and am I the only one that thinks this is a bunch a bull?"

"Cat," Cody intercepted, realizing her control was about to snap. "Don't shoot the messenger."

"Are you ever going to take responsibility for your words and actions?"

"I agree with you!" he shouted.

"That you're an ass?" she purred. "It's about time."

"The mission, Cat, the mission." He closed his eyes in frustration. Lord, but the woman could hold a grudge.

"Oh." She shrugged. Just like that, she released him from her claws. "That's a start I guess. What do you propose we do?"

"I don't know. I'm curious about this Winthrop character. I want to know why the big guy got so upset when he found out about you going after Barrera. I'd also like to know what all of this has to do with today's paper and Atlas's disappearance. The man is our best agent – I find it hard to believe he was taken captive so easily."

"Best agent?" Cat couldn't pass up the opportunity to watch him squirm just a bit more.

"Second best, of course." Cody bowed his head in acknowledgment.

Cat smiled saucily at him. "Thank you. And I missed today's paper."

"The press has found out about Chameleon. Well, not the name of the organization, but some DEA agent talked to Sam Waterly and you guys made the front page of the Washington Post."

"How much do they know?"

"Only that the Cat is scaring the hell out of the underworld." Cody stopped for a moment to turn his restless horse in a circle before coming back to Cat. "This fiend, supposedly a man, most likely has two cohorts. It is unknown if there are more illegal operatives of this nature gallivanting about. There is the remaining question as to which government agency the Cat belongs to and who hands out the orders, not to mention the paychecks."

"That's all?" Cat raised her eyebrows. "Wow. I bet his highness is in a panic."

"I'd say so. They know a lot more than he ever intended, and if someone's digging, they could very well figure out the food chain."

Cat bit her bottom lip and thought for a moment before deciding. "I'll check out this Peyton Winthrop character then continue with the Barrera mission as planned."

Cody nodded his approval. "Check in. I'll let you know if anything new pops up."

"Just don't mention where I am to anyone."

"Do I ever?" He gave her that lopsided grin of his. It took her a moment to realize she was smiling back.

Her brow creased in consternation. "Take care of yourself."

"You too, baby girl," he laughed. With that, she whirled her mount around and urged him into a gallop, leaving Cody to watch her retreating back.

FOOL'S GAME AVAILABLE SPRING 2013

MORE GREAT READS FROM BOOKTROPE

Ring of Fire by **Heather Huffman** (Romantic Suspense) Wealth, beauty and power are somehow not enough. Maybe if you add in smuggling and rare diamonds?

The Puppeteer by **Tamsen Schultz** (Romantic Suspense) A CIA agent and an ex-SEAL-turned-detective uncover a global web of manipulation that will force them to risk not just their fledgling relationship, but their very lives.

A State of Jane by **Meredith Schorr** (Contemporary Women's Fiction) Jane is ready to have it all: great friends, partner at her father's law firm and a happily-ever-after love. But her life plan veers off track when every guy she dates flakes out on her. As other aspects of Jane's life begin to spiral out of control, Jane will discover that having it all isn't all that easy.

Fiery Hearts Collection by **Heather Huffman** (Romantic Suspense - ebook) Heather Huffman bundles three heartwarming and exciting romantic suspense novels about strong and diverse women whose lives intersect as each discovers her unique ability to leave her mark on the world; includes *Jailbird*, *Suddenly a Spy*, and *Devil in Disguise*.

Caramel and Magnolias by **Tess Thompson** (Contemporary Romance) A former actress goes undercover to help a Seattle police detective expose an adoption fraud in this story of friendship, mended hearts, and new beginnings.

... and many more!

Sample our books at:
www.booktrope.com

Learn more about our new approach to publishing at:
www.booktropepublishing.com